I0646668

SINNER'S SANCTUARY
VOLUME ONE

by
MILO ZEPHYR

Edited by Vinnie Corbo
Front Cover design by Tony G
Back Cover design by Vinnie Corbo
Interior design by Vinnie Corbo

Published by Volossal Publishing
www.volossal.com

Copyright © 2024
ISBN 978-1-963359-03-9

This book may not be reproduced or resold in whole or in part
through print, electronic or any other medium. All rights reserved.

Table of Contents

1

TOWN OF CLOWNS
(PART 1)

It was June 13th...Friday the 13th to be specific. Summer break was on and I was feeling pretty excited. My name is Anaya. I'm a college student; a black college student. I attend an HBCU. Pretty awesome for a black female right? School's out for the summer 'til next semester, so I decided to come back home to good ole' Houston, Texas.

Unfortunately, the trip had been long. I was tired and the journey still wasn't quite over yet. 'Traveling tired' is a different typa' tired in my book. I was sitting in the Mississippi airport waiting to depart on my final flight to Texas.

Boarding didn't begin for another forty-five minutes. So to blow some time away, I decided to call my friend Alana who was also waitin' for a flight.

"Hey bih! Gurl, I miss you already!" Alana said answering my call.

"Girl, same here. I'm just waiting to get on this plane. I'm supposed to fly outta here at 3:25pm," I said.

"Gurl you should be thankful your travels are almost over. You only got one more flight, just imagine tryna' get from Florida to California!"

"I know, but you know how I am when it comes to traveling; I *don't* like it! Plus you should be happy. You getting ready to go to where all the palm trees at, where the celebrities be at, and yo parents got that nice-ass crib!" I said, a little jealous.

"Gurl, I know, but that ain't even the point. The point is that I still got at least two more flights. I'm not even gonna look at the itinerary. But you right though, I'm 'bout to be on the beach laid up everyday wit' somebody son!"

"Must be nice," I laughed. "Ain't much in Texas fa' me but food and some old friends. And hold on, I though you said this was a hot girl summer?"

"*Guuurl*, bitches say that all time and don't neva' stick to it... AND I'M ONE OF THOSE BITCHES!"

"Alright then, sis!"

As we started to crack up, my laughter was suddenly interrupted by the sound of the intercom system...

"Attention all passengers, Flight A666 departing to Dallas has been delayed. Departure time is now at 4:30 pm. We apologize for any inconvenience this may cause."

It seemed as if everyone in the waiting area groaned at once. Talk about inconvenience. My flight was set to arrive in Dallas by 4:55pm, but now it was looking more like 5:55pm. Not to mention that from Dallas I was gonna take a bus to Houston that was gonna be like three hours. Now I was gonna miss that bus, *and* the next bus after that too. I'd be cutting it close to get to the station.

That final bus to catch wasn't gonna be until almost eight at night.

"Did you just hear that shit?" I said, pissed off.

"Yeah that's fucked up. Shit, I'll prolly get in the house before you now."

"Don't even fucking remind me! This is why I hate coming back home. For me, nothing ever goes right in the South... hell, it *goes* South!"

"I hate to be that girl, but you *really* thought you ate just now with that pun!"

"I did. Oh, and thank you for making me feel better?"

"Relax, you're gonna make it home and that's all that matters...period!"

"PERIOD!" I emphatically agreed.

"Alright girl," Alana said, "I'll call or text you later... my flight is boarding."

"Alright, safe travels sis!" I said and hung up.

Then, I sit miserably by myself waiting... and waiting... watching TikTok videos... and waiting... until I ended up falling asleep.

I slept for about an hour and before I knew it, I woke up just in the nick of time for boarding. The flight was relatively comfortable as there were only about twenty of us all together. When I finally arrived in Houston, it was 6:00pm.

The bus station was another twenty-three minute Uber ride away. But lucky for me, the final bus wouldn't be coming until 8:00pm.

I really didn't feel comfortable being at this bus for an hour and a half, but I didn't want to bug my parents. That would have just give them something to complain about later.

So I made both a safe and financially irresponsible decision and took a three hour Uber. Yes, a three hour ride with some stranger. My patience got the best of me. I chose convenience over safety.

I opened the app to book my ride. My driver's name was Derek and he was literally only two minutes away. See what I mean when I say convenient? After waiting around for those minutes, Derek finally pulled up.

2

TOWN OF CLOWNS
(PART II)

My Uber driver's name was Derek. He was chill overall and young himself. He had only just graduated college about two years ago. So we talked about college, parties, social media, TikTok, celebrities, how much adulting sucks; you know all the stuff young adults talk about.

We talked for the first thirty minutes of the ride. I scrolled through social media, watched a couple episodes of a show on Netflix, and looked out of the window for a few minutes until I eventually fell asleep after about an hour and a half.

I could feel the rattling of the car as we drove through the empty, quiet roads of Texas. The cool breeze swept around my body, and even with my eyes closed I recognized how the bright sunset was beginning to transform into the night sky. I continued to keep my eyes shut, with slight moments of dozing on and off, until I eventually lost awareness of my surroundings and myself.

I just…drifted away…

I slept 'peacefully', well the most peaceful sleep your gonna get in a car. When I opened my eyes to check my phone, I see it's 8:30pm; which made me feel good because that meant that I would be home in at least an another hour or so. However, I also realized that the car wasn't moving anymore.

"Hey Derek, is everything alright?"

Derek didn't respond.

"Hey Derek!" I said considerably louder.

He still didn't respond and it was honestly starting to aggravate me.

"Yo, can you hear?" I barked.

"Shhhhh!" Derek finally replied.

"Who you shushing?" I asked, slightly offended.

Derek motioned to me. "Just shut up. Come up here and look...but do it slowly."

"What is you talking..."

"Just do it. Trust me," he insisted. "But again, be slow with it."

I was a little hesitant to even trust this guy. After all, he was just my Uber driver. I don't *actually* know him. I identified a daring sense of urgency and fear in his tone, which persuaded me to just listen to him. So I did.

I slowly lifted myself from the back seat, which made me even more nervous considering I had no idea what I was getting out of my seat to even look at. It *is* Texas after all, so maybe it's a bear, cougar, or a pack of coyotes. I absolutely do not like animals; especially wild ones.

But what I saw was something I didn't anticipate in the slightest. A pack... no, as a matter of fact, fuck a pack. I was damn near a community of fucking CLOWNS! People dressed as fucking clowns. They just stared at us. Some smiling. Some with a blank face.

Derek whispered softly. "I think they set a strip of nails out. Our two front tires are popped for sure. I just barely managed to gain control of the wheel. I'm honestly amazed that you slept through that."

So not only was I not making it home any time soon and woken up to a civilization of creepy clowns, I almost died in a car crash *in my sleep*! I was speechless, literally no words to utter even if I wanted to. What do you say? Hell, what *can* you say in this matter?

Suddenly my internal thoughts were broken when we felt a bump at the tail of the vehicle. Derek and I looked back simultaneously and out of thin air it seemed as if a whole other community of clowns formed behind us. The car was officially surrounded. They didn't attack us or anything; at least not yet.

Derek looked at me. "So, uh, any suggestions?"

"Yes, because I definitely have experience interacting with a community of clowns!"

"No need to be sarcastic. I was asking a genuine question. These clowns don't look very friendly and I'm not trying to die tonight."

Suddenly the group of clowns near the hood of the car broke away to form a small path. Another clown walked through the path toward us. This clown was different from the others as he seemed more 'human' than the rest; if that makes sense. He was certainly dressed like a clown. He had a red ball nose, a terrible outfit filled with color, a white painted face with black underlining and bright, bright red lipstick that almost looked more like blood than lipstick.

He approached a vehicle with the hugest, yet most disturbing, grin I've ever seen in my life. His teeth were pearly white and perfectly straight, yet sharp looking. They were more like fangs than teeth.

I couldn't help but feel intimidated, as I knew he wasn't coming to welcome us to the town. It was evident that he was the ring leader of this circus because the rest of the clowns seemed to show him a great deal of respect by the way they moved for him. At the hood of the car he just stared and smiled. In fact, that's what they were all doing. Smiling and staring...

"Do you have any suggestions?" Derek asked nervously.

"I don't know, but I think it's best if we don't move a muscle right now."

"Well we can't just sit here forever, ya know."

"Yeah, I get that more than you could ever understand, but as of this moment they haven't harmed us yet. I think if anything we should just stay calm and allow them to make the first move."

"If we let them make the first move, we might just end up dead! Haven't you seen that movie IT?"

"Now really isn't the time for movie references, this shit is real; *very* real, my friend."

Suddenly the demonic freak show moved closer, surrounding the car. They began marching around us. It was as if they were playing ring-around-the-rosie with our car. They taunted us by making silly faces and creepy smirks. They also began honking horns.

Then I noticed they had knives and machetes; things that I didn't care to see at all. Part of me wanted to take out my phone to record this perplexing madness, but I also considered the fact that pulling out a phone might trigger them. I also considered that I might need it, so I decided to slip it in my bra.

It seemed as if this taunting went on for almost twenty minutes. At this point, I was honestly hoping for them to make a move because this was not only downright disturbing but also very tiresome. The anticipation of what they might do next was really starting to get to me. Should Derek and I just try to make a break for it? Should I just pull out the phone to try and call 911?

As much as the fear was starting to get to me, I figured doing anything irrational could lead to a death sentence. Were they really just gonna march around us all night long? I couldn't see how they weren't tired yet.

As we stayed in the silence of the marches, I took some extra time to observe the appearance of these clowns. Honestly, any clown is creepy enough for me, but for the average person, they weren't exactly Pennywise horrifying. But they weren't Ronald McDonald either. They were almost like any clowns you would see at a kids birthday party, just a little creepier. Plus, they had more dangerous 'toys', of course.

I also noticed the ring leader chose to just stand smiling, as the rest of his union marched around us. This man, if he could even be called that, just *smiled*. He stood as still as a statue. Since Derek was directly in the front and I was in the back, I couldn't help but feel as if he was staring directly at me, and only me!

It made me so uncomfortable that I wanted to just look away. But it's not as if looking out of the left or right passenger windows would make a difference as their were clowns all around us. Even as they marched, their eyes didn't look ahead at all, but rather continued to follow us.

"Hey Derek! Do you happen to have anything as a weapon by chance?" I asked, but Derek didn't respond. "Derek? Hey DEREK!" I whispered loudly with bass, but I received no response.

I moved close to the driver's seat to see what was up with him. He was sweating bullets and his eyes were bloodshot red. It looked as if he hadn't blinked in the last half hour or so.

I nudged him, "Hey Derek! I know you're scared and I am too, but we have to stay calm. The moment we show too much fear, we give them power and they'll only continue to antagonize us."

He still didn't respond. In fact, he didn't move as muscle or even blink. At this point, I didn't know whether to be pissed at him or feel sorry for the guy. But I had to come to realize that we couldn't just sit all night. I didn't think they planned to just roam around us all night and not do anything.

I tried to get Derek's attention again. "Derek, do you happen to have any weapons? I know you said the two tires are blown, but is there any chance we might be able to just make it a mile then walk the rest of the way?"

Still no response. I looked at the GPS monitor in his car. What seemed odd was the fact that it looked as if we weren't even on the map anymore. It even said in blue lettering that the location couldn't be identified.

Derek finally spoke in a very low voice, "We might not be going home tonight."

"I know this is all so scary and so sudden but don't say anything like that."

"We're so fucked. This is fucked up. My girlfriend's having my baby. All I wanted was to make some extra cash for the baby's room..." Derek trailed off as if he was speaking to himself.

He started to break down into tears. I felt so bad for him. He's about to be a father and now he just might not make it home for the birth of his baby. I didn't want to admit that to him, so I tried to reassure him that things would be okay but I don't think it worked.

Derek pulled out his phone. "I just wanna call my girl one last time."

"D-d-d-derek, I understand! But please, please just relax. Don't do anything crazy!"

"NO, I NEED TO SPEAK TO MY GIRL!" he shouted.

"DEREK PLEASE!"

I reached to snatch the phone from him, but before I could, he had already dialed. I could hear the electronic voice through the tiny speaker.

"*The number you have reached is not in service, please try your call another time."*

"Perfect, just perfect." Derek said, angrily hanging up.

Suddenly the marching footsteps paused. If the eyes of these weirdos weren't on us before, they definitely were now. The smirks on their faces dissipated and become faces of anger.

I turned to the front to see the ring leader holding a harpoon gun; a fucking *harpoon gun*!

"We're fucked, we're fucked, we are so done for," I said in a panic as he started to take aim.

"DEREK GET DOWN!" I screamed loudly

But before I could even get my complete sentence out, a spear shattered through the glass and into the skull of poor Derek.

The shattering glass shook me but what really set me off was Derek's blood dripping all over me.

"AAAHHHH!" I screeched at the top of my lungs.

I had blood on my face and in my hair.

The next thing I knew, the car started to fill with a gas of some sort. Crying and hyperventilating, I started to slightly puke. I tried telling myself to hold my breath, but there was too much tension in my body, mind, and spirit to direct focus to one single thing at this moment. I started to get cold, dizzy, woozy, and my vision started to get blurry.

"STAY UP, STAY UP, STAY UP!" I exclaimed internally.

But that wasn't enough. Like I knew I would, I started to fade more and more until a cloud of darkness was all I could see. All I wanted was to go home for summer break but it looked like *that* would not be happening anytime soon.

Normally, by this time of night, I would've showered and been scrolling through Netflix looking for a horror movie. Instead, I found myself in one. This could end up being a really long night or a really short one...

3

TOWN OF CLOWNS
(PART III)

I woke up groggy. I could still see the veins on my head pulsing a thousand miles a minute. It felt as if someone had knocked me in the head with a bat and I damn near almost forgot where I was and what the hell had happened.

As the blurry vision I was experiencing started to fade away, my memory came back real quick when I realized that I was in a fucking circus. There was a community of psycho people dressed as clowns in the bleachers.

What really seemed to wake me up was seeing the face of the devil himself; the bastard who killed Derek. He still had that same creepy-ass smile on his face. He held a microphone in his hand.

I tried to move my body but something was restricting me. I looked down at my torso to realize that I was tied up. I tried wiggling my hands and feet, but those were tied up as well. I really had no means of escape.

It was really loud in whatever twisted circus this was supposed to be. I looked over to the left and right of me and saw that there were two other people tied up; a girl and a guy. I wonder how long they've been here?

There was also someone else tied up. Except she wasn't tied in a chair like me and the two other people. Instead, she was tied to a spinning wheel. If that wasn't bad enough, her mouth was gagged and she was stripped completely naked.

Finally, the creepy head clown spoke into his microphone, "Gooooood evening folks! I'm August, your faaaaaavorite clown in the town!"

The audience roared with applause.

"Please help me welcome our two returning guests, Sonya and Tyler!"

They clapped and whooped again.

"We also have a new guest tonight," he announced as he slowly walk towards me.

"Now little lady, won't you go ahead and introduce yourself to the customers tonight!"

For a moment, I froze and I wasn't even going to respond. But then I realized how quick Derek was killed from one wrong move, so I figured maybe it would be safer to just play along with his game.

"Annnn...Anaya...my name's Anaya."

"Well, well, well, Anaya," August taunted. "You should feel like a really special guest tonight. Here in the town of Paysino we get lots of folks from different strokes, but it's not everyday we get a guest like you!"

I didn't know what the hell he exactly meant by that shit, but I assumed it had something to do with my race. He was right though, you don't usually see someone like me get in situations like this. I'm definitely just a chick that got caught up in the wrong place, at the complete wrong time.

"Well, lucky for you, tonight you get one of the best shows ever. For tonight's first act, our participant Jennifer will be spun around and eventually get to have a 'hands on' experience with Biscuits and the family! Although she may not live to relish the moment!"

The crowd roared with laughter.

Poor Jennifer started to wrench into tears. Sadly, it was obvious what was coming her way.

"Alright, enough with the introductions. It's time to get this show going! Am I right?"

More loud cheers from the crowd.

August pointed and shouted, "SPIN THE WHEEL!"

The audience chanted, "Spin, spin, spin..." as the wheel began to circle.

At first, the motion seemed to be rather slow. There were two people (well, clowns), standing there preparing to throw sharp objects at Jennifer. One was a girl that looked like a rip-off Harley Quinn. She was possibly no older than eighteen. She stood next to a table of knives.

There was a guy there too. He was ugly as hell and as big as a walrus. Someone you definitely don't want a confrontation with. He had pickaxes in hand.

The girl was first to through. She threw one of her knives and just barely missed the eye of Jennifer.

"Aww I missed, no fair!" she whined.

"Relax," August replied. "You'll have plenty more chances to hit the bull's-eye, Tiffany"

Of course this bitches name was Tiffany. Figures.

It baffled me how they could casually converse about injuring a human.

The big guy then proceeded to throw one of his pickaxes. I flinched presuming it was about to go straight into Jennifer's brain. Fortunately, it missed by mere centimeters. I breathed a sigh of relief.

I thought for sure that was going to hit her. I couldn't even imagine being in her shoes right now.

"It's alright Clubba," Tiffany shouted to him. "You'll get the next one. I'm sure!"

The wheel started to spin again, this time a lot faster. I honestly didn't know if Jennifer's chance of survival was higher or lower from the increase in speed. Tiffany then used all the force in her body to throw one of her knives.

This time, it hit Jennifer's right arm.

"URUHHHhhh!" Jennifer screamed.

As blood rolled out of Jennifer's arm, the wheel started to spin again. This time it went even faster. I noticed that Jennifer started to gag from the speed.

Clubba threw his next weapon. He got her in the lower stomach. Jennifer screeched in pain.

As the wheel stopped, blood, sweat, tears and puke dripped off it and on to the floor.

"Damn it," Tiffany bitched. "Clubba got a good part!"

August wasted no time. "SPIN THE WHEEL!"

As the wheel began to spin again, the crowd went wild. This time my basic human eyesight couldn't focus enough to keep up with the amount of speed going on with this spin.

This time there was no rest. Clubba and Tiffany relentlessly threw sharp objects at Jennifer's body.

I couldn't keep up with it all, but I definitely saw one knife go into Jennifer's chest, another knife hit her right leg, and finally, a pickaxe in the skull.

This go around, Jennifer was definitely dead.

"And the winner of tonight's festivity is CLUBBA!" August exclaimed.

As the crowd cheered, Jennifer's body was removed from the wheel and dumped on the ground right next to my feet. I almost puked at the sight of her body. It was riddled with knives, axes, blood, puke and God knows what else. I've never had asthma, but I certainly couldn't breather right then. I desperately tried to seek a breath. After all, this bitch just witnessed two deaths in one night.

"COME EAT, BISCUITS!" Tiffany hollered.

Next thing I knew, a fucking tiger, a wild ass *tiger*, came out and completely mauls anything left of Jennifer.

Her body was next to my feet so I just knew I was about to be Biscuit's next snack. This woman not only got spun and stabbed to death, but she also is being eaten alive (well, dead), before my very feet.

August addressed the crowd. "Alright folks, we're gonna take a quick intermission to get our lovely couple Sonya and Tyler prepared for their first live act! Ah, so wholesome right? Like an early Valentine's Day!"

" Awww!" the audience clamored.

"Ahhh, how romantic," Tiffany sneered.

"But that's not all, August continued. "Tonight our newest guest, Anaya, will get to perform her first act as well!"

"Wooooo!" the crowd cheered.

August turned to me and said. "Look at all the rewards you're getting on only your first day here, Anaya. You got to meet two new friends, you took a ride in an overpriced Uber, you got a front row seat to witness Jennifer's turn on the wheel, *and* you got a up close meet and greet with Biscuits. You've truly been rewarded a premium vacation!"

"Aw, I'm so jelly," Tiffany giggled sarcastically.

What really got me was that August actually believed the words he's saying. He was right about one thing; this *has* been a very 'premium vacation' that I would never forget. Hell, I might not even get the chance to remember it as it seems I'll eventually be a participant in the festivities. I definitely did not enjoy being a 'special guest.'

Next thing I knew, me and this Sonya girl were being wheeled into the back by some clown guards. Once we reached the back, they began applying clown makeup to our faces. Once they completed the makeup, they dressed us as freakish girl clowns; skirts and all.

Once they finished toying with us like their dolls, they ran off somewhere. I figured this would be the perfect time for me to talk to Sonya to see if I could get some information from her.

I looked toward Sonya, "Hey, you good?"

"No. No, I'm not good," Sonya cried. "My boyfriend and I came to Texas for a light vacation. Our car broke down and we ended in a town of clowns; where I just watched a naked, innocent chick get murdered and her remains eaten by a tiger called Biscuits! So *no,* I'm not good."

"What can you tell me about Jennifer?"

"She ended up here three days before my boyfriend and I got here. She was on a work trip and was on her way back home to her family. She was supposed to be marrying her boyfriend and father of her children in two weeks. Now that man won't have a returning fiance' and the kids won't be getting a returning mother."

"Since you got here, have y'all tried anything to get out?"

"There weren't really any opportunities to. Most of the time, we were locked up in the equivalent of a prison cell. Before Jennifer died, she and I discussed the possibility of being put in some sort of circus games; we're dealing with clowns after all. So we figured that during the period of preparation like now, we could try to fight our way out."

"Well what's stopping us from doing that right now? I'm sure for whatever activity they've got planned for us, they will at least have to untie us from the chairs. They have the two of us here together so we might be able to take out those two clown chicks just before going on stage."

"I don't know if it's a good idea," Sonya cringed. "Not sure I wanna piss them off any further!"

"Okay, so do you wanna just wait to be killed! Either way, it's obvious they have no intentions of keeping us alive in the long term. After they kill us, they're just gonna get more victims. Hell, they may have even more stored away."

"Jennifer told me she participated in another act before we got here. Not every act is fatal," Sonya said with hope.

"Okay, but did she or did she not just get spun, stabbed, and eaten in front of our eyes tonight? We will be killed just like Jennifer in the long run if we don't do something soon. I don't know about you, but I'm not tryna' become Biscuit's next fucking biscuit!"

Sonya paused for a minute before responding. "You're right. I have some strength left. When the clowns come back for us, we'll take those crazy bitches out! But I intend on saving my boyfriend too!

"Gurl, I'm not telling you not to. I understand," I emphatically responded.

But the truth was, if it came down to it and she screwed everything up trying to save her boyfriend, I would ditch the both of them. I'll be fair for now, but at the end of the day, I've gotta put myself first. I already had a close call with Uber driver, Derek!

After about five more minutes or so, the two clown chicks came to get us. They untied our legs, removed the roping from our torso, but left our hands tied.

Sonya and I nodded at each other. That's when I smashed clown chick number one in the face with the back of my head. Clown chick two started to get on high alert but Sonya was able to smash her forehead to forehead. She then proceeded to choke her with the rope tied on her hands. I did the same to my girl as well. We pulled the rope tightly against their throats until it was obvious both were dead or at least unconscious.

I realized one of them had a knife in their pocket. So I managed to pick it up with my two tied hands. I cut the roping off my hands first, then cut Sonya's.

"Let's go find your boyfriend and cut him loose," I said.

"Sounds like a plan!" Sonya agreed, as we sprinted out of the room.

We knew Tyler couldn't be too far away considering they had planned to have us all perform (or should I say, die) together.

The setup reminded me a lot of a circus of course, but also of a school drama class backstage set up. They sure had a big budget for psychotic, murderous ass clowns.

We made a right down a passageway where we saw one male clowns with Tyler.

I heard the clown murmur, "I don't know what's taking them so long. We have to get them on stage."

The clown was facing away from us and his attention was on holding Tyler. He did not see me coming when I snuck up behind him with the knife and slit his throat. As he fell to the ground spewing blood from his neck, Sonya ran to Tyler.

"Babe.... how'd ya get out?" Tyler said groggily.

"It doesn't matter right now. I'll explain later. I'm gonna cut you loose so we can get out of here."

Once Tyler was cut loose, we were now grouped as a trio preparing to escape.

"Do either of you possibly know an easy way out of here?" I asked.

"Actually, when they brought us in, I do remember going through a set of red cage-like doors. I think some of the staff members might actually have a set of keys to unlock them," Tyler recalled.

Hearing that, Sonya checked the guy I just killed and by the grace of God, he had keys.

Sonya held them up. "Got 'em. Thank goodness, lets get out of here."

"Uh, uh, uh...not so fast!"

We turned to see Tiffany smiling menacingly.

I wasn't too worried about her because I knew I had a knife. Plus, I figured the three of us could take her out together if it came down to it.

But my bravery melted when I saw Clubba approach behind her. It was definitely time to run now. So that's what we did.

It seemed as if Clubba and Tiffany were sprinting just as fast behind us. We ran straight ahead. It seemed as if the doors were a universe away. As we ran, Tyler fainted, tripped and fell to the ground.

"Oh my God, Tyler!" Sonya Screamed, proceeding to turn back to help Tyler.

"Y'all come on! They're literally on our fucking heels!" I shouted.

Tiffany and Clubba were now less than a hundred feet away from us.

Tyler opened his eyes and spoke in a soft voice. "I'm very weak. I don't think I'm gonna make it. Just keep the keys and go..."

"No baby," Sonya cried. "Just come on and fight we're almost there!"

Tiffany and Clubba were too close for comfort now. Since Sonya had the keys, she was preventing my escape.

"Come on Sonya," I shouted. "We have to go NOW!"

"NO! TYLER, BABY!"

And as I pulled her away for the run, I briefly glimpsed back to see Tyler take a hatchet to the skull from Tiffany.

"AHHH, TYLER!" Sonya screamed.

We continued down the hall as fast as we could. Both of us were sweating through our stupid clown makeup. When we finally found the red gate that led to the outside door, Sonya stopped.

" I can't. I'm going back for Tyler!"

"Sonya they are right behind us. You can't!"

"Yes I can, and I am! You're the reason I couldn't be there, you made me leave him for dead!"

"I'm trying to save you. Besides, he wanted you to leave!"

"Doesn't matter, I'm going back!" Sonya insisted.

Clubba and Tiffany were too close. This was matter of life and death now. Sonya had the keys in her pocket, so I snatched them from behind her.

She didn't notice because she was frozen in fear standing face to face with Tiffany and Clubba. She managed to turn around hoping to escape, but I was already on the other side of the gate. I knew it was too late for her. I had no choice. I locked the gate behind me.

Sonya shouted, "YOU EVIL BIT..."

But she was interrupted as Clubba grabbed her from behind and proceeded to bear hug her. He was so big and strong that his squeeze pushed the air out of her. Then I heard her bones crack.

As Clubba dropped Sonya's lifeless body to the ground, I ran to the door leading outside. When I finally got outside, it was still very dark, but I just kept running straight until I couldn't anymore.

I ran for about fifteen minutes straight until I eventually came to a gas station. I ran inside crying and freaking out with my clown makeup and all still on. I told the guy behind the counter what happened.

He gave me some water and called the cops. They came pretty quickly and took me to the police station. I wasn't very confident explaining everything to them because I knew there was a high chance they wouldn't believe a word I was saying. But I tried my best to explain everything.

Officer Danica took my statement then said with a smirk, "Sweetheart, you mean to tell me killer clowns killed your Uber driver, gassed you unconscious, took you to a place called Paysino where they dressed you up like this?"

"Yes," I exclaimed. "And I also witnessed them murder three other people. I'm not making this up. Isn't my outfit evidence enough!"

"There is no such thing as Paysino." Officer Patrick interjected. "There is no town in Texas with that name!"

"I swear to God I'm not..."

"Look sweetheart," Officer Danica smiled. "We know it's summer break so y'all students are getting wild. Just get your things we're gonna take you home!"

"But I witnessed three people get absolutely slaughtered today! I almost died! I'm not about to be told I'm crazy or that I imagined that!"

"Okay then, do you have proof of these *killer clowns* you speak of?" Officer Patrick questioned.

As the officer asked me that, I realized the I had my phone on me the whole time and didn't take a single video or photo. Fuck."

"Well...not exactly," I said.

"Our point exactly," Officer Patrick replied. "Young lady, please just grab your things so we can take you home. Don't get yourself into trouble you can't get out of."

It was at this point I realized it was pointless to argue with them any further. It was obvious they didn't believe me; and I really can't blame them. If I were on the opposite end of this, I can't say I would downright believe someone telling me about a town of psychotic clowns.

What freaked me the most, was the fact that neither myself nor either of the cops had actually ever heard of this town. That combined with the fact that Paysino didn't even show up on the GPS map in the car with Derek.

Was this town simply just a town none of us had ever heard of? Or was this town some sort of weird supernatural ghost town?

The more I pondered on it, the more painful my headache grew. Again, I don't know how I ended up in that insane town.

I wish I could tell you to avoid a specific road, or not to take a certain exit, but I can't. All I can say is, just try to avoid driving late at night in Texas. You don't want to end up in the town of Paysino.

I don't feel great about the 'tactics' I used to survive, but I did what I had to do in the moment.

Enjoy summer while you can, my friends. It always ends quicker than it came. Because August *will* come... soon enough.

4

REINCARNATE
(PART 1)

"Beep... beep... beep..."

The morning alarm woke me to the rising sun of New York. I brushed my teeth, cleansed my face, and showered. I dreaded going to work. I scrolled through a little social media, booked my taxi and headed off to my corporate job for eight hours. Live just to work another day, right?

My name is Daria, by the way. I'm just a twenty-four year old girl working in fashion; specifically fashion marketing. I'm single, no kids, no boyfriend and I seldom interact with my family. Everyday just feels like another day and to be quite honest, I'm just not satisfied with my life.

Sometimes I wonder what it would be like to be someone else; even if just for a day. And yeah, yeah, I know, my life could be worse, and that I should be grateful for the life I have, even if it's boring. But a girl can dream, right?

I mean haven't you all pondered being someone else at least once; whether it be Ariana Grande or Heather the girl next door?

There's so many of us in this world and we all live different lives. Different lives to the public, different lives at home, and even different lives in our own head. But I guess all we can do is make the most out of the hand we were dealt by the almighty, right?

After a fifteen minute taxi, I got to work at eight in the morning, sharp. I went to my computer to check some emails, looked to see what meetings with what departments I had for the day, what work I needed to complete, etc. You know, the same old high-paid corporate stuff. Honestly, the best part of my life is my job which is probably why I work so much.

"Rise and shine, bestie!" my friend Sarah tooted.

"Sup Sarah! I was actually just about to text you to see if you got in yet. Wanna head down for daily iced coffee?"

"Is that even a question, of *course* I do!" she exclaimed.

Sarah was my work bestie. We've been working together for two years since I moved to New York. She's been a good thing in my life. Although, she's very loud and sometimes way too outgoing in the morning.

"So I went on a date this weekend!" Sarah boosted with a smile.

"Oh yeah, I remember you telling me about that. How'd it go?"

"Well, his family is very rich. He's very hot, such a hunk. But there were a couple of red flags, unfortunately."

"Red flags?" I questioned.

"Well, he went to the bathroom and I don't know what made him think it was a smart idea to leave his phone at the table with me. I know I shouldn't have been invading. I actually didn't sneak or anything. But a message popped up on his phone, and it said wife!"

"So he's married?" I grimaced.

"I'm assuming," said Sarah. "I wouldn't even be surprised if he has a kid too! When a man tells one lie, they're most likely telling multiple."

"Well that's what you get for trying to seek love on Tinder!" I joked.

"Ha! Well, it's 2023. No one actually interacts anymore. Doesn't help people like you that are already introverted. It just gives y'all an excuse to be more lonely."

"Well, excuse me if I don't wanna just walk up to a stranger and basically ask them if they're trying to fuck!"

"I know, but Daria, I'm really worried about you. You seem more depressed than usual. Just like anyone else in this world, you deserve to be happy, love, and be loved. Come on you can't stay lonely forever."

I blushed. "Oh my God, you sound like my Mom now. She's been pressing me to get a husband for a while."

"The problem is you're waiting for this perfect moment to happen, where this perfect man, the knight in shining armor, is gonna come swoop you away. This isn't Disney, sis. People have flaws. Things will not always be perfect and you just have to accept that," Sarah said emphatically.

"Okay! Enough preaching! Are we still going to the BTS concert this Saturday?" I asked, trying to change the subject.

"Of course we are, but are you doing anything tonight?"

"No. Why? Is there something you wanna do?"

Sarah made a villainous smile. "Well, there's a guy on Tinder that I'm friends with. I think he's really your type. And I think you should try and hangout with him! He thinks you're really cute."

"Um, boundaries?" I said. "Did you send this guy a pic of me or something?"

"Yes. I know, I know, I should've consulted you first, but I knew you wouldn't even give it a chance if I didn't get it in motion already."

"So you agreed *for* me?" I remarked. "To go on some kinda date with this guy?"

"Yeah, yeah, sorry. But he *is* really hot, though!" she exclaimed as she showed me a picture of him.

Okay. I gotta admit. He was honestly really, really attractive; almost devilishly handsome.

"So what do you say?" Sarah pushed.

"Fine," I surrendered. "I guess I don't have anything else to do tonight."

"Yes!" Sarah said, victoriously. "I'm telling him right now. You're gonna get sum tonight!"

"Slow down. I'm not promising him anything tonight. And since you're the coordinator of this date, where are me and mister Damien meeting?"

"You guys are going to be meeting at Krsytal's Club. You're welcome!" Sarah said sardonically.

"Thanks," I said, even more sardonically. "Thanks for setting me up on a date on *my* behalf."

"I know. Again, I'm sorry but I just can't stand to see you so miserable. Just have a good time tonight. Even if it's just for this one night. Please!"

"Sure, whatever. But I'm still not giving up on the possibility of marrying Taehyung."

"Trust and believe. Jungkook will be mine when it's all said and done!"

"Oh my god, it's the simping for me!"

"It's the TikTok lingo for me, but duty calls. Lets head back up before we get our heads ripped off."

We laughed as we took the elevator for work.

•

The day went on as normal. I had my meetings, responded to a crap ton of emails, had lunch with Sarah, went back to work, got the finished sample of my scarlet dress I was pitching to my bosses and stakeholders, and before you knew it the day was over.

I couldn't deny the fact that all day during work, I couldn't stop thinking about my upcoming date with Damien. I was actually really excited to meet him and see where this goes. This might just give me something to live for again. Ya know?

5

REINCARNATE
(PART II)

8pm came pretty quick. It was now time to meet Damien at Krystal's. I gotta admit, that picture of him was cute and I *was* interested to see him in person.

I called my Uber up, it came, I went, and I arrived. Krystal's was as busy as usual. The hot one hundred hits blasting through the speakers per usual.

I texted Damien. Sarah had given me his number during lunch. He had already gotten there like ten minutes before me. I found him at a back booth and frankly, he was even hotter in person.

He was twenty-four like me, he had tattoos on his arms, a buttoned shirt that was unbuttoned at the top, brown hair, and gorgeous brown eyes. I was actually a little nervous to even talk to him. It felt as if he was almost a little out of my league. But there was certainly no turning back at this point.

"Damien?" I asked shyly.

"Hey, that's me!" he exclaimed, then got up to hug me.

"I apologize that *we* are just now getting to communicate

with each other. My friend decided to play love doctor." I joked awkwardly.

"Well I'm glad she did. You're really pretty! Daria and Damien. I kinda like the sound of that!"

"Thanks, and yeah I guess it does have a nice ring to it!"

"Yeah, so what do you do for a living?" Damien asked.

"I work in the fashion industry. I do marketing but I have designed pieces myself!"

"Nice, that really suits a cute girl like you. I'm a fitness coach. I have clientele that I oversee their fitness and dietary health!"

"Well, that definitely suits someone like you!"

"Oh so you've been checking out my muscles!" Damien flirted.

" I mean, yeah," I admitted. "I feel like it's only fair that I flatter you some, considering you've been so flirtatious with me."

"Hmm… so you're a girl of equal opportunity. I like that. Most chicks expect the male to do and be everything. They don't believe in giving compliments. They just like receiving them."

"Well, I can assure you that I'm not like most girls; not to sound cliche," I assured him.

"You're not," he assured back. "I guess that's why I felt drawn to you in the first place. When Sarah sent me that pic of you, I knew there was more to you than meets the eye. You just need someone to help shine your lights a bit. Girls like you are hard to come by. That's why you're a real treasure!"

"OH MY GOD!"

"My bad, was that too much!"

"Kinda," I laughed. "But I'd be lying if I said I didn't like it a little!"

We both laughed and from there, shot, after shot, after shot was being ordered. We continued to just laugh and talk about casual stuff like work, TikTok, etc. He even told me he had plans on becoming an influencer; which I'm not gonna lie, was kind of a turn off.

He even managed to convince me to get on the dance floor with him. He was definitely not a good dancer but neither was I. So we looked like two weirdos dancing in the club together. But for us, nothing mattered anymore. It was a vibe. It felt like it was just the two of us in the club.

For the first time in a while, I was actually happy to be myself. We even ended up sharing a kiss in the strobe lights. I was having so much fun, that I started to lose track of time.

Eventually, I somewhat came back to my senses and realized that I still had to get up for work early in the morning. So I decided that as much as I didn't want the night to end, it was time to go home.

"Well thanks," I told him genuinely. "I really had a good time tonight!"

"I did too," Damien quickly agreed. "I'm really glad we met. "Ya know, the fun doesn't have to end just yet!"

"I know, but this is the life of being another product of the 'working-til-you're-sixty-years-old' system."

"How're you getting home?" he asked.

"I'm just gonna call an Uber."

"No, come on, let me take you home."

"No, it's cool, you really don't have to."

"I want to," Damien insisted. "You came out for me. Let me take ya!"

I gave in to him and let him take me home.

When we arrived at my place I said, "Well, thanks for bringing me home. You really didn't have to."

"It's cool," he said. "It's really not safe to be riding late at night with an Uber driver."

"Do you wanna come in for a sec? Maybe for like water or to use the bathroom?"

"Sure."

So we went up to my apartment together.

"Nice high rise ya got here," Damien said, impressed. "The view is amazing!"

"Yup, this is my sanctuary!"

"Well, thanks for inviting me in, I feel honored!"

"You should. I don't do this very often. You should be *grateful!*" I teased.

"Oooh, it's always the quiet ones that have a feisty side. Don't worry though, I *am* grateful that you let me in. And I fully intend on showing you that!"

"And, how do you exactly plan on doing that?"

Before I knew it, Damien and I were body to body, tongue to tongue, and soul to soul. I won't go all erotica, but let's just infer the rest. What I *will* say, is that this was the best feeling in the world. It felt so rewarding to be touched and pleasured again. He took me somewhere I hadn't been in awhile. For thirty minutes of my life, he took me to the sky and showed me all the stars...

•

I awoke at two in the morning. After coming over the woozy feeling from drinking, *and you know what else*, I began to slowly come to my senses. I wondered if Damien had left or not since I had fallen asleep.

It didn't take long to discover that he didn't, as I now realized that he was physically standing directly over me. It really creeped me out.

Through the bright late night lights of New York City, I could make out the outline of a knife. I wanted to scream, but I couldn't. I wanted to say something, but I couldn't. Not only because he had his hand over my mouth, but because I was literally speechless.

The next thing I knew, I felt a sharp object go into my stomach, not once but multiple times. The pain of my flesh being shredded, the smell of blood, my life flashing before my eyes... Soon it felt as if I no longer even felt the pain. It felt as if I was now just watching my body be slaughtered.

My throat, my head, my everything; it was heart breaking to think that I had given someone a chance, I shared things with this person, I gave my body to this person. For a second I even fell a little in love with this person.

I never thought that death could be this painful. I was a fool. I honestly don't know what hurts more, the physical pain of this death or the emotional pain of betrayal. After all, I wasn't happy anyway. I guess I was glad to have a moment of happiness, even if it was short lived. Goodbye cruel world...

•

"HONK!!!"

"Sir, can you please wake up! I have other people to go pick up. Get out!" a cabbie shouted at me as he honked his car horn.

I awoke with cold sweats.

Wait! I just realized, I woke up! I started touching all over my torso. Nothing was wrong. I was definitely alive. But I remember being killed last night. Why was I still alive? Why was I in a cab right now? And most importantly, why did that cabbie just call me 'SIR'!?!?

There were so many questions running through my head.

"Sir! You have a job and I have a job. Could you please get out!"

"Stop calling me a man. I'm not a man!" I protested.

"I don't care what the hell you are, just get out!" he yelled as I exited the cab.

He had taken me to some building. Somewhere I was not familiar with. This was definitely not where I worked. My head was pounding like crazy and I'm was so confused.

Suddenly I saw Sarah passing by me across the street.

"Hey Sarah!" I exclaimed.

She just looked at me like I was nuts and kept walking. So I ran across the street toward her.

"Hey Sarah, it's me Daria!"

"I don't know a Daria, and I don't know you. So could you please leave me alone!"

"What do you mean?" I asserted. "It's me, Daria, the girl you've been working with for two years!"

"Again, I don't know any Daria," Sarah proclaimed. "I've never worked with a Daria. And I certainly don't know you. Besides, you definitely don't look like a Daria!"

"Sarah, wait!" I pleaded.

"Sir, if you don't leave me alone, I will call the cops!" she threatened as she stormed away.

What did she mean she didn't know or worked with a Daria? Why did she call me sir? Why was I still alive after being stabbed to death? What the hell is going on?

I ended up going into the building the cab driver dropped me off at. I need to get to the restroom as soon as possible. I felt sick.

When I walked in, a lady at the front desk greeted me!

"Welcome back Dominic! How was vacation with the family?" she asked.

" I'm sorry, did you just call me Dominic?"

" Yes? That's your name right?"

"Yes, yes, that's my name sorry!" I responded then walked away to avoid making the situation any more awkward than it already was.

I finally found a bathroom. First, I threw up. Then I went to the sink to rinse my face. I listened to my voice. It was deeper and definitely the voice of a man.

I raised my head to look in the mirror. I was, in fact, a man. I had a mustache, facial hair, and broad shoulders. Everything you would expect of a man.

I checked my pockets. Sure enough I found a wallet that had an ID. My name was Dominic Canatello; a thirty-three year old business consultant.

There were also labeled pictures in my wallet. Apparently I had a wife, named Kaitlyn, and two kids; a boy named Mikey and a girl named Allison.

I still didn't know how to soak this all in. Why was I still alive? Why was I now a man? And why didn't my best friend even acknowledge my existence? Did I even exist anymore? Did I *ever* exist?

Only time will tell. I figured I'd have to continue to live as Dominic Canatello for now. I have to accept that Daria is a thing of the past, for now... or maybe forever.

6

REINCARNATE
(PART III)

The day had been absolutely terrible. I died the night before and woke up in a man's body. I had facial hair and a penis, a wife, two kids, and my best friend didn't even acknowledge my existence.

While at 'work' today, I went on the computer and accessed my old company's website. They have employee pages that show our department, education, and the project designs we've worked on. But guess what? I was nowhere to be found anywhere on the website.

I even tried texting my sister's number. Of course, she too, had no idea who I was. She also had no idea who 'Daria' was either. It's like I didn't even exist anymore.

Now what? Was I was supposed to go on living like some middle aged man with a wife (which I'm *not* into by the way) and two kids? I didn't understand why any of this was happening. I didn't know what to do. It's not like I could have just gone back to being Daria, especially if she never even exited in this timeline of the world.

Maybe I had no choice but to live on as 'Dominic.'

So yes, basically the day had been horrible and I already hated my job and my life.

During the day, I got a text from my 'wife' saying she would pick me up after work. To be honest, I've never been with another woman before in my own life, so I didn't know what to say when she arrived at the end of the day.

"Hey babe," Kaitlyn said. "How was work today?"

As she leaned in to kiss me on the lips. I tried to turn my head as fast as I could. Unfortunately, I didn't turn it in time. Oddest sensation in my life!

"Oh wow! Dodging my smooches today, that's not usually like you."

'Yeah, cuz I'm not actually your husband,' I thought to myself.

"Well anyway, dinner is almost ready. I've already got the kids started on their homework. Mikey's teacher called today. She said he was talking a too much in class."

She just kept going on and on. I was completely zoned out. I'm no better than a man.

"Dominic? Babe! Are you even listening?" Kaitlyn grilled.

"Sorry babe, it's just been a really long day at work."

"Aw, I'm sure it has. Well, you got two hot meals waiting for you, one at the table *and* one in the bed!" she exclaimed excitedly while biting her lip.

I nearly puked and cringed simultaneously hearing those words coming out of her mouth. It was definitely something a middle-aged MILF would say. I had no idea how I was supposed to live as Dominic... 'til death! (Well, actually my second death...)

We finally arrived at the house. I'm going to be honest, while I don't hate kids, I don't exactly like them either. I never even had my own kids, so this was going to be quite the adjustment.

"DADDY! WELCOME HOME!" my 'daughter' Allison shouted as we walked through the door.

"H-hey sweetie. How are you?" I tried to act like a 'dad.'

"Daddy, guess what's in two weeks?"

"Your birthday?!" I took a guess.

"No. Mommy's birthday," Allison corrected me.

"Oh, oh yeah right," I tried to play it off.

I looked over to my 'wife' Kaitlyn. She looked a little hurt and aggravated. She smiled at Allison.

"Come on, Allison, wanna help Mommy with the salad?"

As Kaitlyn took Allison in the kitchen, I was about to run upstairs, get in the shower, and cry about how I was now a middle-aged man. But Kaitlyn stopped me.

"Sweetie, your not gonna greet your son?"

"Oh, right. I almost forgot!"

So I went back down the steps to find my 'son' Mikey at the table doing what looked like to be his homework.

"Hey little man!" I said, hoping it sounded natural.

It didn't because Mikey said, "Dad, I'm eleven years old. I'm not a little man!" He actually sounded a little aggressive.

"Excuse me young man! Just who do you think you're talking to like that?" I said very femininely while moving my head around. As I did, both the kids and Kaitlyn looked at me like I was crazy. Oops, I had to act like a 'man.'

"I mean, calm down champ!" I said trying to self correct, but when I realized what I actually said, I cringed.

"I'm sorry Dad. I just wish you didn't work so much."

Kaitlyn interjected. "Mikey, Allison, head up to your rooms for a minute. Dinner will be ready soon."

As they left, Kaitlyn took a seat. I guessed it was time for 'dysfunctional family talk.' She looked serious.

"Dominic, I've warned you about this a long time ago. I understand you work a lot but you still have to try and make more time for the kids. I work a lot too. It might be time for us to plan a family vacation. Maybe lets hit that beach house you were talking about this summer."

She went on, and on, and on, and on some more.

As she kept talking, I just kept staring dumbfounded. All I could think about was, 'How the hell could I have been stabbed to death, come back to life with no records of my existence, into a thirty-something year old man with a wife and two kids. I was just a twenty-four year old woman that drank Starbucks everyday, worked in fashion, and scrolled through TikTok. I was supposed to be going to a BTS concert this Saturday, but now I'm going to be playing 'Dad' and 'Husband' for who knows how long.

"Oh my goodness, Dominic! Again, you're not even listening to me. What's going on with you today? You've been acting very strange!"

'If only you knew,' I thought to myself.

I figured she would just keep nagging me if I continued to show a lack of concern. Actually, I really didn't care. I didn't know these people. I didn't marry this woman and birth these kids with her. But I also know what it's like to be a woman dealing with men.

"I'm sorry babe. Like I said, it's been a really long day. We should definitely go on that vacation this summer. And haven't I told you, but you absolutely fabulous today!"

"Aw, thanks babe. I'm glad you're so understanding!"

That did the trick.

"Of course. And after dinner, I will go pick up some ice cream for dessert as a surprise for the kids!"

Kaitlyn beamed. "That would be great. I just know they'd love that!"

She stood up and tried to kiss me again. I tried to divert.

"Wait. I'm not that clean right now. I wouldn't want you to get any germs!"

"Since when did you become a germophobe? Besides, aren't we gonna spread a lot of germs tonight!" she teased erotically. God, I prayed I didn't have to sleep with this woman tonight. I'd literally rather die again.

We had dinner about an hour later. I showered for forty-five minutes. Not gonna lie, I cried in the shower the entire time. I'm still a female at the end of the day.

Kaitlyn made meat loaf, mashed potatoes, green beans, dinner rolls, and a side salad; definitely a very 'middle-class family' dinner. The food itself was not my taste, but it did feel good to be laughing, talking, and having dinner with others. I didn't live with people in previous life as Daria.

I didn't know anything about this family and I didn't know who 'Dominic' was before I took over his body. But they definitely seemed like a good family. Unfortunately, I didn't know how prepared I was to take on the role of a husband and father; let alone be a man. At the same time, I didn't want to leave these kids without a father.

After the meal, I told the kids about the ice cream and they were excited. So Kaitlyn gave me the car keys and I used the GPS on my phone to find a store nearby. I figured this would give me a chance to have some alone time to really think about things.

I really didn't want to live as Dominic. I was a woman, not a man. I couldn't be a husband or a father. I was a young woman in a man's body. I didn't know how to be a husband or father; even if I really wanted to.

I just wanted to be me again, to be Daria again. Could you imagine waking up as someone else one day? And even worse, in a world you never knew existed? No one remembers you; not your job, best friend, or sister.

I was angry at that bastard Damien for killing me. I wanted to hunt him down but would it really even make a difference? He probably wouldn't know me anyway?

I knew that I'd probably never be able to be myself again. I knew I needed to except it but I just couldn't. I didn't know if this was the universe's way of giving me a second chance at life, but I thought I would've rather died as myself than live as someone else. As much as it hurt, I guessed I would just have to live on as Dominic.

I went into the store, grabbed the ice cream and decided to head back quickly because it was getting late. I really wished there was a way that I could just go back to being myself, but I decided that I was going to live this life the best that I could as Dominic. My father and I didn't have the best relationship as I got older, so maybe I could be the father that I wanted my father to be for Allison and Mikey.

Thinking about it that way actually motivated me a bit. So I made up my mind to wipe the tears off my face, go inside, and make the best damn ice cream cones these kids ever had.

When I pulled up, I noticed that all the lights in the house were off. This was weird because when I left, Kaitlyn was doing the dishes while Mikey and Allison were watching television waiting for me to return with the ice cream. I tried the door and it opened with no hesitation. It was pitch black inside and so quiet you could hear a pin drop.

"Guys, I'm back," I announced. "I got the ice cream."

As I turned toward the kitchen, I saw puddles of blood running from the kitchen to the living room. I dropped everything in my hands. The ice cream and cones fell to the ground.

I started panicking. I didn't know what to expect. Blood definitely wasn't a good sign. I rushed through the dining area and into the living room. There on the couch, the kids laid dead. There was blood all over both of them. They had obviously been stabbed multiple times.

Then I saw Kaitlyn. Her torso had slashes and stab wounds. Even worse, her head was smashed into the screen of the television.

"Oh my god, oh my god, fuck, fuck, fuck!" I started panicking and sweating.

What was I supposed to do? I couldn't just leave or I would be an automatic suspect. I was not going start my new life as a man by going to jail.

Suddenly I heard sounds coming from upstairs. I crept up the steps as quietly as I could. It seemed as if the sounds were coming from Kaitlyn's bedroom. In that moment, I realized I had no weapon. I thought about going back downstairs for something I could use, like a knife. But I decided to keep going.

When I got to her room, there was no one in there. I checked under the bed and in the closet. Nothing. I *knew* I heard footsteps from this area.

I checked the bathroom too. Again, there was no one to be found.

Then, on the ground, I found a finger, I should've known better than to even waste my time bending down to grab it. It was the worst mistake of my life because when I stood back up, I saw someone standing directly behind me in the sink cabinet mirror.

They wore all back cargo-like pants, an all black hoodie with a vest, and a very creepy theater face themed black mask. They held a scythe-like weapon as if he were the grim reaper.

Before I could even think about running, the guy lunged towards me with his weapon. Again, I could see my death happening before my very eyes. At least it was quick this time. My head came off clean and blood sprayed everywhere. I guess no more Dominic, no more Kaitlyn or kids. What a short lived life, huh...

•

"Sayaka, Sayaka, Sayaka! Wake up right now!" I heard as I awoke to the sound of an angry woman shouting. She was calling me Sayaka. She wasn't speaking English but I could still understand her for some reason.

When I was able to regain full eyesight, I realized I was in a classroom; a classroom full of what looked to be Japanese high school students. The angry woman was Japanese too.

"Sayaka, I tried to wake you up!" a young girl said.

"Quiet Mizuru!" the woman interjected.

"Yes Ma'am!" the young girl responded, sarcastically.

I couldn't believe what was happening. I died again last night, I was killed by some guy in black. He murdered that whole family. Kaitlyn, Mikey and Allison. I remember it like it happened yesterday; because it literally did!

Why was I back to life again? Why was I killed again and by who? Why the fuck am I a Japanese high school girl now? What the fuck is...

"Oh, so now you think it's okay to not answer a question when a teacher is asking you Sayaka?" the woman scolded.

"Ms. Makima, sleeping beauty didn't get enough beauty rest!" a boy in the class joked causing the whole class to laugh.

"Quiet Kai, you already have detention after school today. Don't make it worse. And as for you Sayaka, since you think it's okay to fall asleep in class and ignore a teacher while being spoken to, you will be staying after school with Kai today for cleaning!"

"Come on, not with her!" Kai protested.

"QUIET KAI!" Ms. Makima shouted.

The class fell silent and she went back to teaching. All I could do was just sit there. I was alive again but I also remembered everything again.

I lost my life as Daria, then as Dominic, and now I'm in Japan as a school girl named Sayaka. As if being murdered twice, losing my identity, becoming a man, witnessing the aftermath of a three family massacre wasn't enough... I'm back in fucking high school!

7

Reincarnate
(Part IV)

My name was now Sayaka Munagi. I was a seventeen year old Japanese school girl. I had been murdered and brought back to life twice. I never really wanted to be a man, husband, *or* father, so in a way, I was relieved to be a female again. But I certainly wasn't expecting to be a teenager; let alone in Japan.

I felt absolutely terrible that family I was just with was murdered for something that really didn't involve them. But then again, I wasn't sure it even mattered in this new timeline. I had no idea who that guy in the hoodie was that murdered me and the three of them. I decided to just call him Grim Reaper.

I decided then, that it just couldn't be coincidence that I was repeatedly being killed and reincarnated into someone else. I contemplated if Grim Reaper could be Damien since he murdered me the first time. Then again, I wasn't sure that really made any sense; not that any of this really made any sense.

The way things had been happening, I wouldn't be surprised if I was to be killed again. It was certainly time for me to be more on guard from now on. I need to do my best to avoid being put in situations that would make me vulnerable; even if there are others around me. The previous events showed that these killers didn't care at all about hurting others in the process; even kids.

"Sayaka are you okay?" Mizuru asked. "You haven't even touched your lunch!"

"Yeah I'm good," I replied. "I've just got a lot on my mind, that's all."

"I understand, especially considering that now you have detention and you have to clean, and even worse, you're gonna be stuck with that asshole Kai."

"Don't remind me," I groaned. "Besides, I'm not going to that detention anyway. I've got *other* things to do!"

"Are you sure that's a good idea?" Mizuru pressed. "I wouldn't want you to get in more trouble, considering how bitchy Miss Makima can be."

While myself and what I'm assuming is supposed to be my best friend in this life, Mizuru, were talking, we caught a glimpse of Kai and his fellow group of losers pointing and looking at us. I seriously didn't have time to deal with a boy all stuck in his feelings."

"Ugh, Kai is so annoying! Mizuru exclaimed. "He's been picking at you all year. It's like he's completely obsessed with you. I wouldn't be surprised if he totally has a crush on you! If he wasn't such a dick, he'd actually be kinda cute!"

"Not interested," I said flatly.

"Also,' Mizuru continued. "If you don't mind me asking, did you have a nightmare? You started jerking and mumbling. When you were finally woken up by Miss Makima, you were panting and sweating like crazy!"

"Actually yeah I did! I had just got my head sliced off!"

"Ahh, ohh, okay..."

Suddenly Kai and his gang walked up to our table.

"Hey, can't wait to clean with you today!" Kai snickered. "Don't worry, I'll take out all this trash, including you too!" he added sarcastically.

His little gang of side chicks started laughing.

"Wow, you thought you did something!" I shot back. "Look kid, I don't know who Sayaka was before, but this is a different bitch speaking right now. I know you think you're 'the shit' right now cuz you haven't lived in the real world with real consequences yet. You may think it's cute to bully a female because you're experiencing your first little crush, but this isn't my first rodeo and I'm warning you right now. Leave me the fuck alone, because I don't have time to deal with your bullshit right now!"

I can tell my spiel startled Kai. He got flustered. So he and his little gang walked away. I sat back down, and although I wasn't really all that hungry, I knew I had to eat for the sake of energy. I felt like being in that big-ass school after hours was another possible set-up for me to die again; and I was tired of dying.

The physical and emotional pain was just too much to bear. Plus waking up as a new identity each and every time made it worse. I knew I might just be delaying the inevitable, but I figured if I could get out of this school today that would at least give me a shot at understanding the situation and figuring out some possible counter measure.

Mizuru and I sat and ate quietly. Soon, it was time to go back to class.

•

I found my desk and noticed there was a note of some sort on it. At first, I was thinking it was Kai and his friends trying to be funny. But when I opened it the note, it read:

"NO MATTER WHO, I WILL ALWAYS FIND YOU"

It was written in what looked to be blood.

"Oh my gosh, is that Kai again!" Mizuru shouted.

"No," I assured Mizuru. "Don't worry about it. It's nothing."

I didn't need her causing a scene in class. I felt nauseous after reading it. It was clear that Grim Reaper had a motive and was waiting to kill me again. It was crucial for me to get out of that school. The rest of the school day went on as normal. Well, as normal as it can be for a high school student. After what seemed like dozens of classes, it was finally time to go home at 3:30pm. I grabbed my things and Mizuru and I started heading to the exit. We made it through the six flights of steps and we're only a few feet from the door when Mizuru asked me again.

"Are you sure it's really a good idea for you to be skipping detention?"

"I *know* it's not a good idea, but at this point in time, I have no choice but to take chances!"

Mizuru had no idea what I was talking about. Freedom was mere inches away, but before we could finally walk out the door Miss Makima appeared.

"Nice try, Sayaka!" she snapped. "Attempting to skip detention. Now, I'll be writing you up as well!"

She motioned to Mizuru.

"Unless you have extracurriculars, go home, Mizuru! Sayaka, you can come with me!"

"Good luck, Sayaka. Text me later!" Mizuru said as she left.

'Sure, sure, I'll probably be dead by then,' I thought to myself.

I considered just making a break for it, but I figured in the event that I would have to continue in this identity as "Sayaka," I might want to tread lightly. I figured I could find some kind of weapon and stay with someone in the case that Grim Reaper appears.

•

I arrived back upstairs with Miss Makima. She had Kai and I in the classroom with brooms, dustpans, rags, and all types of other cleaning supplies.

"Kai," she said. "You should already know the drill by now. Sayaka the two of you are expected to be here for two hours. Floors must be swept and mopped, windows cleaned, and all desks wiped down. There will be no talking. I will be here supervising. Maybe if all goes well, I might let the two of you go home thirty minutes early."

Miss Makima then sat down at her desk. Kai rolled his eyes at me and we got right to cleaning.

Kai and I had been cleaning for about forty-five minutes when I realized we still had at least another hour to go. So far so good, though. There hadn't been any sign or a potential opening for Grim Reaper so far.

"I have to use the bathroom," Miss Makima announced. "I'll be right back you two. Same rules still apply!"

Miss Makima disappeared to the bathroom while Kai and I continued to clean.

"Hey, Sayaka?" Kai broke the rules by speaking.

"What do you want?" I replied, realizing I was breaking the rules too.

"Just wanted to apologize for being a dick to you this whole year."

"Oh, so just cuz I put you in your place, now you wanna be nice?"

"Honestly, it was unexpected and it was kinda hot. But you were right. The reason I've always been a dick to you is because I actually really like you!"

"So that's your way of telling Sayak… I mean *me,* that you like me?"

"I know it wasn't right to do it that way, but I just wanted you to notice me!"

He suddenly put down his rag and started to move closer.

"Sayaka… will you… go out with me?" he asked.

He started to lean in to kiss me, but even in the body of a seventeen year old, I'm not kissing a minor!

"BANG, BANG, BANG!"

Suddenly there was the sound of three consecutive slams or bangs of some sort. Come to think of it Miss Makima had been in the bathroom for a really long time. I had a very bad feeling.

"What was that?!" Kai jumped.

"I don't know, but I'm gonna go check it out."

"No," he said. "You stay, I'll go instead!"

"No," I disagreed. "I think it's better if you stay for now, it's a female bathroom anyway."

"Right, I didn't think of that. I'll come with you then!"

"What? You gonna be my protection?" I teased.

"Hey, can't blame a guy for trying!"

"Whatever, let's go."

Kai and I went down the hall to the women's staff bathroom. The door was slightly cracked open, as if someone just entered or left. Kai stayed outside as I walked in. It didn't take long to find blood... and Miss Makima's body. Her face was caved in. It was like she barely had a face anymore. I lightly vomited at the sight. It was absolutely gruesome. I ran back out to the hall to Kai.

"WE NEED TO GET OUT OF HERE NOW!" I shouted.

"What do you mean? What did you see?"

"Miss Makima has been murdered, we need to go!"

"Holy fuck! Shouldn't we call the police?"

"We don't have time for all that right now, he's near!"

"Who's near?"

"HIM!" I responded pointing at Grim Reaper down the hall. This time he had a sledgehammer in hand.

"WHAT THE FUCK!" Kai screamed.

I grabbed him and yelled, "RUN!"

Unfortunately, the only exit I knew of was six flights of stairs down. It's the only shot at survival we had. Thankfully there was a staircase leading down that could get us to the exit, so we took that one of course. As we were heading through the flights of stairs, Kai lost his footing, tripped and twisted his ankle. He yelped in pain.

To be honest, I didn't feel like trying to hold him up, but I couldn't just leave him to die either. I tried dragging him but I only had the body of a short teenage girl; just not quite strong enough to really get too far, even with my adrenaline pumping.

I managed to drag him the last two flights to the exit, but Grim Reaper had already arrived. With the strength of a true demon, Grim Reaper swung the sledgehammer, knocking Kai straight in the back of the head. He wasn't dead, but he definitely had a serious head injury.

I felt that I only one option, and that was to make a break for it. As guilty as I felt, I let go of Kai and made a run for it. Grim Reaper stood above body of Kai. I looked back momentarily. Kai had his hand out.

"Please...help...me," he cried out softly.

Grim Reaper then picked up his Sledgehammer and smashed Kai head until there was nothing left. As I was running, I actually started crying. Not only because I was scared and afraid of dying again, but because it was so horrifying to see all these people killed, even though I didn't know any of them very long.

After another five minutes of running, I finally found another back exit, but it was locked. I was very unfamiliar with this part of the school. I had no idea which way to run next. I decided to just go right, hoping for the best but not ten steps later, I came face to face with 'him.'

He smacked me in the face with the sledgehammer. I don't think I even need to explain the rest. I knew the drill by now. He brutally smashed my head into pieces. I could even see small pieces of my brain.

Maybe I deserved this death. I left that boy to die. He cried out to me for help. Whether his death mattered in my next life or not, it was still something I would feel guilty about forever.

This death was my karma. But I made the decision as I faded, that the next chance I got, I would make that son of a bitch pay. I was going to fight back. I may not ever be able to be Daria again, but decided that in my next life, I would make it worth living!

8

REINCARNATE
(PART V)

It's been three days since I first died and so far I've been four different people in my lifetime. I lived most of my life as Daria, a single twenty-four year old woman working in the fashion industry.

I was murdered by my one-night-stand, Damien, and awoke as Dominic Canatello; a thirty-plus male with a wife and two kids. The entire family, including myself, was brutally murdered because of me.

Next, I awoke as Sayaka; a seventeen year old Japanese school girl. My instructor was murdered, as was a boy named Kai who had a crush on me. I felt guilty about Kai because I watched him get murdered and did nothing to save him. I was then murdered myself, by a sledgehammer wielding Grim Reaper.

This time, I awoke as Carlos Ramirez; a twenty-year-old college student that still lived with his parents and his sister. It was the same drill as the last two lives. I woke up and went through the day living as this other person.

This time would be different though. This time I intended to not die again; at least not by Grim Reaper, or by the hands of anyone else for that matter. This time I was gonna take this son-of-a-bitch by surprise. This time... I would be killing him.

I didn't know why he was after me. It's one thing being killed myself (hell I had already died three different times), but innocent people being killed was just fucked up, even if it didn't matter in the next life I went to.

The physical and emotional pain of dying over and over by itself was unbearable, but watching others die is another beast by itself. It was something I didn't think I could continue to endure, so this time I decided to be ready to fight back.

Besides, I'm wasn't sure if this 'reincarnation thing' had a limit of how many times I can could back. After two times of going through the trouble of finding me, killing anyone around me, before killing me made it obvious that Grim Reaper had no intention on letting me live through *any* of the identities I took on.

I didn't know how this was all happening. Why was I coming back to life? Who was this man hunting me down? Something had to give. And I just want to live.

•

I went through Carlos's normal day routine of school and sports. Apparently I played football, so I got to join in on practice. The locker room smelled horrendous. I don't know how males do it.

After practice, I came home, had dinner, and prepared for the night to end. I was very nervous, tense, and heavily on guard. I even have a knife under my pillow.

I repeatedly looked out of the window. I also bought a ton of energy drinks to stay up all nigh.

"Bro you good?" asked my sister, Valentina.

"Yeah, just a little stressed, that's all."

"So stressed that you have a bunch of energy drinks in your room? You haven't said a word to me all day? And you have a knife under your pillow that you did *not* cover very well."

"Sorry, I know that's probably not like your brother. The Carlos you once knew."

"Uhh, what do you mean by that? I get your an English major, but chill out with the philosophy this late."

"No I'm being serious. Can you talk for a minute?"

"Sure," Valentina said. "I'll pull the door up some."

She pulled the door up some and sat down on the bed with me.

"Alright, what's going on with you bro?"

"I don't expect you to believe me. But I'm not your brother. I'm actually a female named Daria. I was murdered and was 'reincarnated' as your brother."

"What?"

"This isn't the first time. I was also reincarnated as a Dominic Canatello; a man with a wife and two kids, and as Sayaka; a seventeen year old Japanese schoolgirl.

"What happened to them?"

Dominic and his family were all murdered. Sayaka was also murdered along with a classmate named Kai and her instructor Miss Makima. I believe the Canatello's, Sayaka, Kai and Miss Makima were all murdered by the same man. I call him Grim Reaper. He has been hunting me down for some reason.

As Sayaka, I was murdered yesterday at around 5pm, and I woke up this morning as your brother Carlos. Don't ask me any 'how's, what's, or why's' cuz I simply don't know. But what I do know is that Grim Reaper is coming back and if I'm not ready this time, I will die again and you and your family could be in danger!"

"Wow, I don't know what to say!" Valentina said shocked.

"I know, I don't expect you to believe me."

"No, I mean I can't say I one thousand percent believe you, but I do know my brother and I can tell you're not him. It doesn't seem like your lying. This isn't the type of joke my brother would make."

"I know this might be a lot to take in, but I'm tired of dying, and I'm tired of seeing others die. I know I'll never be Daria again, and that's still not easy for me to accept..."

I started to break down into tears.

"...Imagine being murdered, losing your identity and any sense or evidence of you existence... being killed over and over, feeling your body parts be cut, seeing the lifeless bodies of an innocent family, witnessing the death of a teenager, then waking up as someone else..."

I cried even harder and started ranting.

"Living *their* life, being with *their* family, doing *their* activities, working *their* job. The only one that remembers your own existence is *you*! It's hard... a-a-and I just can't take it anymore!"

I sobbed and continued to ball my eyes out. I had been trying to put on a strong front all this time, but I just lost it. You really don't realize how valuable something is until it's gone; especially when it's your own life.

Valentina was sympathetic.

"I'm sorry," she said. "I don't know how to react to all of this really, but what I can say, is that I could only imagine what that would feel like. I love being *me*. There's no one else that can be me and I can't be anyone else. Look, I still can't say completely believe you, but I'll assist you in anyway I can, at least for of safety myself and my family. Either way you still have my brother's body."

"I appreciate that," I said calming down. "For starters, is there any situation that you can think of in Carlos's life that could be unpredictable, or anything that would possibly make Carlos vulnerable?"

Valentina thought for a moment.

"Nothing that I can really think of. The only thing that could be vulnerable might be that Mom and Dad are leaving for their second honeymoon this weekend!"

"Well, there's still a chance he could show up tonight. But if he's sticking to a pattern, he will come tomorrow more than likely!"

"Okay, well is there anything else that might help?"

"Yes, were you going to be here this weekend?"

"Well I wasn't gonna be gone the whole weekend, but I did plan on hanging at a friend's."

"Well can you stay this weekend?"

"Uhh..."

"Come on, you said you kinda believed me!"

"Alright fine, I'll stay!" Valentina conceded. "Do you have a time in mind?"

"Not really, but I know he's gonna want to catch us by surprise. So it'll probably be really late, probably between ten or twelve at night."

"Okay, well the plan is set then," said Valentina. "I really hope you aren't playing around, Carlos!"

"I wish I could say it's all a joke!"

Valentina decided to hang in my room for the night. We kept watch together, but she still ended up falling asleep. So I stayed up from dusk 'til dawn by myself.

The parents left the next day around 11:00am. Valentina and I didn't really leave the house. We just ordered food, watched TV, and talked about girl stuff. I definitely think she was starting to believe me.

Before we knew it, it was eight o'clock, then nine, then ten. I was starting to get really nervous. I could tell Valentina was as well. We discussed the plan one last time.

"Carlos," Valentina asked one last time. "If you really are my brother and not Daria and this is all a joke, please say something now!"

"Again, I'm not. But I really appreciate all your help and thank you!"

"No worries, even if you aren't my brother on the inside; you're still him on the outside."

"Not just for staying and helping, but also for calling me Daria. That's the first time someone's called me my name in what feels like years."

We then discussed how we were going to shut off everything in the house, except for maybe the living room TV, to make it look like we we're asleep. We figured he was more than likely going to come in through the back door. We decided to hide in Valentina's upstairs closet in her bedroom, because her room is closet to the steps.

The time was now 11:45pm and we're still sitting in her closet. Valentina was starting to get a bit antsy. She was starting doubting me.

"I swear to God bro," she threatened. "If you lied and I missed the party and stuff..."

"Girl just have some patience. If I was lying, I wouldn't have made up a whole as story, cried to you or went this far?"

"No," Valentina said. "I'm done with this I'm leav..."

"Smash, smash, smash!"

We heard the sound of glass being shattered.

"OH MY GOD!" Valentina cried.

We faintly heard the sound of the back door being opened. As he came in, you could hear the sound of heavy footsteps, and things being moved around below us. I guess he figured we weren't in the kitchen or the living room, so he started up the stairs.

Valentina started to pant heavily so I covered her mouth. I was breathing kinda hard myself. He was inching closer, and closer, and closer to the door every minute. He actually walked past her door first to go check the other rooms, I assumed.

He then came back around to her door. He paced around in her room, looking under the bed, ripping the bed up from sheet to cover. Then he came to the closet.

I was ready to go for his legs with my knife. Valentina had a taser, spray, and a knife of her own. The moment of moments was about to begin. Slowly, he opened the door...

3 Weeks Later

Valentina and I managed to take down Grim Reaper. It wasn't easy and we certainly almost died, but we did it. I don't want to relive the fight scene between the three of us, so I'm just going to keep it simple. He attacked, we fought back, and we won. What happened to his body? Well, it just sort of dissolved and disappeared leaving us with a trashed bedroom to clean up from a fight only the two of us will ever know about.

After the fight, Valentina was really in shock. She was now forced to accept that her brother was gone. She now knew that everything I told her was true. She took it hard.

Not only did this poor girl help me kill someone, but her brother as she had known him all her life was truly gone.

We've kept all this between us, and even though it's not my fault, I still apologize to her everyday that I can't be her brother; the male she grew up with. She says she understands and I believe she does. I can only imagine how that must feel being on the other side of this.

Since then, I've been trying to get myself accustomed to Carlos's lifestyle. I've learned how to live as someone else, and how to be a male in general. No matter how much I try, I just can't force myself to want to be with another female; even if I'm now in a mans body. That part has been a nightmare within itself if you catch you my drift.

This is the first time since I've reincarnated that I've actually had time to sink in and adjust myself to a new everything. I know I need to let go of Daria, but it's just not that easy to do.

For weeks I assumed that Grim Reaper was gone. At least I did until three days ago. I was on campus and found a note on my desk that said, "STILL HERE." Was that from 'Him?' I also couldn't shake the recent feeling of being watched.

My 'Dad' has been acting very strange lately as well. I was doing dishes yesterday evening when I could've sworn he said something along the lines of, "You can't escape..."

Escape what exactly?

Tonight he said, "I'll always follow you..."

I'm not sure what he means by that but it's not a good sign. I'm not sure how much longer I may get to live as Carlos. But one thing I am sure of, is to always appreciate what you have and who you are.

I crapped on my own life, and now look at me. There's no one better to be than *yourself*.

You can't cheat death, because in the end, he always gets his lick back...

9

SATAN'S HOUSE:
THE MAESTRO FAMILY

'Ughhh! Another day of this stupid job,' I thought.
I really should've went to college. Maybe I should still
go. This job was annoying, having to drive around in the
summer heat from door to door to random people's houses.
But that was the life of a salesman.

I didn't feel college was for me. I always heard my
parents and others talking about job opportunity and how the
earnings for a salesman was growing rapidly, but I wasn't
feeling it. Okay, the pay was decent when you got people
to actually buy your shit. But I was seriously starting to
question my life choices.

Oh, the name's Jericho by the way, and again I'm a
salesman... that didn't go to college. When I first graduated
high school, I didn't think that college was for me. My Uncle
was a car salesman and I always heard the old folks saying it
was a good job to go into, so I gave it a shot.

I worked for Stone Corps, a company that sold
kitchenware; my specialty was *knives*. Honestly, the job

itself was not difficult. It was actually easy money when you could get old folks to sign up to buy a set. But be prepared to get a lot of 'no's' and deal with some real pricks.

On this particular day, I was a little excited because I got assigned to some suburbs in Boston Massachusetts where typical middle to high-middle class families resided. So I knew I was gonna make some bank over the next two days. If you were living and working in Boston in 1957 you had it *made in the shade*; as they said back then.

When I arrived in suburbia, I got right to work. However, it definitely wasn't what I was expecting. The residents were pretty nasty and gave me the royal shaft. Some simply didn't answer the door or just told me to 'go away' in my nicest words to describe it.

I kept getting no, after no, after no. I knew I wasn't gonna get everybody, but *damn*; not even the few old folks were trying to hear it. As the day went by, I started to get more and more discouraged to the point where I was just ready for my shift for the day to end, even though I had made no money.

It was now around 7pm, so the day was basically over. So much for the suburb payday, right? I still had one more house to go to and that was the Maestro family. Honestly, I was tempted to just skip them and go home for the day, but I figured maybe, just maybe, I'd get lucky this time.

When I got to the house, something about it spoke to me. It was a really nice house but it felt off for some reason. It gave me a bad feeling. When I got out of the car and started making my way to the front door, it felt as if somebody was watching me through the window curtains. I even caught the tiny glimpse of a wide, creepy grin in the window.

"KNOCK, KNOCK, KNOCK"

I lightly knocked on the door and I waited for a minute. No one answered. I figured maybe this was a sign from the Lord to just walk away, but then the door opened.

"Good Evening young man, what brings you here to the home of the Maestro's?" Adam asked.

"Oh, I'm sorry to bother you, sir," I replied. "I was just making my last round for the night and your house was on my list. I work for Stone Corps. My company sells kitchenware. My name is Jericho. I'm here to market our refined, cutting-edge knife set."

"Is that so?" Adam smiled. "So your a salesman?"

"Yes I am."

"That's a very competitive industry for a kid your age, ya know!"

"Please don't remind me, sir," I said shaking my head.

"How many have you sold today?" he asked.

"To be frank; none. So if you'd like to buy a set, that'd really make my night!"

"Ain't that a bite! Well today's your lucky day, Jericho. We're having dinner and my wife was just about to cut the cherry pie. Why don't you come in. We can try one of your knives out with the pie. We'll all have a bite and I might just buy! How does that sound?"

"Well sir, if you and your family are having dinner I don't want to intrude or interrupt," I said politely.

"No it's okay son, just come on in. You don't mind right Eva?" he shouted to his wife.

Suddenly, a gorgeous woman with burgundy hair appeared.

"Oh, of course not, sweetheart. I certainly don't mind at all! Jericho, ginchiest young man aren't you," she smiled.

"Oh, thank you ma'am!" I said a little flustered.

Eva was insanely gorgeous. I couldn't help but stare.

Adam noticed and said, "Jeez Jericho, take a picture won't cha!"

"My, my, my apologies sir!" I stammered, embarrassed.

"No need to, my boy. Wanna fuck her?"

I couldn't believe he just asked me that. His face got longer and darker; almost slightly demented. I wanted to believe he was joking, but it didn't seem like it, so I just tried to laugh it off.

After awkward silence, Adam said, "I'm just joking with ya, son!" as the kool-aid smile reappeared across his face.

I just laughed it off awkwardly but my face began to hurt from so much fake cheesing.

I went in with them and I gotta admit, they had a pretty nice pad! Newest television on the scene, nice fully furnished kitchen, and big living room area too! I noticed they had a lot of pentagram shaped things scattered around the house. I don't know much about that typa stuff, but I heard that was the Devil's symbol.

"Go ahead and have a seat at the table, Jericho." Eva gestured. "I'll bring the pie in just a minute!"

"Will do ma'am!" I said as I sat down at the table.

I was instantly startled by the presence of two children. They both had on masks. The masks were all black and had an upside down smirk for a mouth. The children just sat there, silently. I know kids are sometimes shy, but something about this was just off.

Adam introduced his children, "These are the Maestro kids; Gabe and Jane. Kids, please welcome our guest. His name is Jericho!"

They waved in a slow motion fashion. I just waved back.

"So, um, are you guys fairly religious?" I asked feeling them out.

"Yes, we go to church every Saturday," Adam affirmed. "We take pride in serving our God. After all, he keeps this family flourishing. He keeps our government flourishing too!"

"Saturday?" I was a little confused. "Are you guys Jehovah Witnesses or another denomination of some sort?"

Adam paused, "Are you religious, Jericho?"

"Well, I come from a family of Christians, so I guess you could say that. But I'm not some super holy guy that tries to be perfect. At the end of they day, we're all human and every sinner was once a saint."

"Interesting take," Adam said. "See, that's what makes our religion different from most; especially Christianity. Our God recognizes that no one is perfect and that humans are inherently sinners. He doesn't condemn us for our dirty deeds. He also gives us all a chance to succeed, as long as we give our entire devotion to Him and auction off some of that moral compass where Christians miserably continue to fail. As long as we are willing to make sacrifices, give our full devotion, follow our contract, and idolize his emblem, we will always be affluent!

"I'm assuming you worship a different type of God?"

"Correct!"

"And if I may ask, what type of sacrifices do you make to your God?" I asked Adam as a twisted grin appeared across his face. He didn't get a chance to answer as Eva had walked towards the table with the fresh baked pie in hand.

"Alright guys," she interrupted. "The pie is done and ready to be cut!"

The children proceeded to clap their hands.

Adam motioned toward my bag, "Well, it's time to test out your product, Jericho. Shall I cut now?"

"Please do sir," I said still hoping to make this sale.

Adam cut into the bright red cherry pie. He then cut the pie into five slices and proceeded to plate the slices.

"I'm very impressed, Jericho," he said. "Very sharp and offers a very precise cut. It'll be good to cut up things with right guys? "

"Of course honey!" Eva agreed.

"Yes father!" Gabe and Jane said simultaneously. This was the first time they actually spoke.

They all started to laugh together. It made me quite uncomfortable. At this point, I was honestly just ready to go.

I tried to make a smooth exit and said, "Well thank you for inviting me into your home, I appreciate the pie offer, but I must take my leave now."

Adam stopped me saying, "Well, we love the knife, I still need to pay you, right?"

Anxious to get out of there I said, "Please, just consider it a token of my appreciation."

"What about my pie, sweetie. Don't you want to taste it?" Eva said seductively, as she proceeded to dip her finger in my slice of pie.

She then scooped a small dollop of the pie with her finger and pushed it toward my mouth.

"Please, I'm really okay..." I said, pulling away.

"Just open up and taste," Adam said. "Don't be difficult now, Jericho!"

Suddenly he was behind me, caressing his hands across my shoulders. As much as I didn't want to, I recognized the potential danger I was in, so I opened my mouth. Eva put her finger in my mouth and I sucked the condiments off of her finger. She then took her finger out of my mouth and proceeded to lick it; disgusting.

"It came out almost perfect, not too many bones this time!" she said as she licked her finger.

"You did amazing honey, I can't wait to taste it later," Adam said.

"Wait. What do you mean bones?"

They turned to face me. Eva, Adam, and the children cackled with laughter. I didn't see what was funny. I had no idea what I had just ate.

I puked a little as it became clear that this family was nuts and what I just ate was definitely *not* just crust and cherry filling.

Adam got serious. "Oh, cut the jig, Jericho! I told you we have to make sacrifices to our God. Pies are an easy way to show our gratitude to the object making that sacrifice possible."

Now I knew what he meant by sacrifice, as well as why they had all the pentagrams. This family was worshiping the Devil and the sacrifices they make are murders of something or someone!

I'd had enough and this time I was not requesting my leave, I was just taking it. I hurried to the door as fast as I could, but it was locked. I turned to look around me and the family was starting to close in on me

"You weren't dismissed yet, Jericho," Adam commanded. "You shouldn't behave like this when we invited you in our home!"

"Please, just let me go," I begged. "I won't say anything about your family or what you guys do!"

"That's very kind of you, but your an important piece required for tonight's ritual. Our God is calling and we can't just ignore that."

Figures in black and red robes appeared and along with the Maestro family, the entire group move toward me. They moved in closer and closer, until all I saw was darkness...

8 Hours Later

The Maestro Family reveled in the temple with the rest of the Maestro relatives to praise the birth of a new era of success, affluence and prosperity. All as one they celebrated, praised, danced, ate and drank. The lifeless head of Jericho lay across the altar, and the scent of fresh baked pies began to fill the area.

Adam spoke aloud to the group.

"Tonight, family, we enter a new era with our Lord by our side. We will see new strides in our prosperity, new investments, new opportunities, new influence for our family, our friends, and our neighbors. We thank not only our God for presenting us with these opportunities and this success, but to our catalysts that make this possible. I raise a toast to Jericho!"

"TO JERICHO!" everyone praised aloud.

"The pies are done! "Adam announced. "Please, dig in!"

THE END

10

DIAMONDS ARE FOREVER
(PART 1)

I had a difficult decision to make. Do I just up and leave? Do I wait for someone to kill them? Or do I kill them myself?

You might be questioning why I'm considering killing anyone, but let me explain. I'm not just some madman that has completly lost his mind and just wants to kill people. No, I'm actually a really sweet guy with a great job, nice home and a loving family.

My wife's name is Eubi. We have two daughters, Luna and Myna. We also have a son whose name is Ruko. We are your typical traditional family.

My name's Yokami Kaminawa. I never imagined I'd be in the position that I'm in right now. But here I am; contemplating murder. I know, it seems crazy. Allow me to start from the beginning...

8 Weeks Earlier

It was a sunny day in Yokohama, Japan. My wife Eubi, my eldest daughter Luna, younger daughter Myna, and young son Ruko were preparing to venture off on a trip to South Korea to visit my wife's relatives for a couple of weeks.

"Ruko, put your toys away," Eubi said. "Or if you're going to bring them, just bring them. We have to hurry off to the airport!"

"Do we really have to be there for three weeks?" Luna asked. "Can't we leave a little earlier?"

"Luna, this is your family," replied Eubi. "Don't be like that. Isn't that right sweetie?"

"I gotta agree with my baby girl," I disagreed with my wife. "Do you guys really have to stay that long?"

"Now don't you start, Yokami. I've planned for this since last fall and we've already discussed this!" Eubi fired back.

"Daddy is scared of being alone! He's gonna see ghosts!" my other daughter Myna joked.

"Daddy's not scared. He's just a little timid of being lonely! Besides I'm gonna miss my little sweetheart!" I exclaimed as I started to hug and kiss her. "I'm also gonna miss you too big boy!" I shouted excitedly as I pick up my five year old son, Ruko."

"Alright sweetie, it's time to go now!" Eubi announced.

As bittersweet as it was, I agreed. We loaded up the vehicle and headed off to Haneda Airport. We got there in about forty-five minutes which was about an hour before their flight departure. As much as I wanted to sit with them a little more, I knew they still had to get their boarding passes, check their bags, and go through TSA. I grouped them in for a hug one more time!

"Alright," I said. "Have a good time guys. I'm gonna miss y'all!"

"We're only gonna be gone for a few weeks, stop being dramatic!" Luna snarked.

"Could you hug us any tighter daddy!" Myna joked.

"Alright, love you sweetie, we'll be back before you know it!" Eubi said as she kissed me goodbye.

Together, they headed off to check-in. I stayed for another fifteen minutes to ensure they made it to the gates squared away. When my wife texted me that they made it, I took my leave. The car ride back was so quiet, quieter than it's ever been in my car since having a family. I can't deny I was a little thrilled initially. The thought of having the house to myself was kind of exciting to an extent, but once you have a family you get used to noise and always having someone else around.

When I got back home, I really didn't do much. I bought some takeout, showered, and watched a couple of movies on Netflix. Before I knew it I was out like a light.

I was awoken around twelve in the morning by a call.

"Hello?"

"Good Morning; is this Yokami Kaminawa I'm speaking with?" the operator asked.

"Yes?"

"I'm calling to confirm your relationship to Eubi Kaminawa, Luna Kaminawa, Myna Kaminawa, and Ruko Kaminawa."

" Yes, those are my wife and kids!"

" Sir, I just want to offer you my sincerest regrets at this time," the operator said in a sad tone.

"REGRETS? Regrets about what?"

"Sir, I understand this may be frustrating especially at this time of night, but there has been an unfortunate accident on flight B621 to Seoul, South Korea. The bodies of your family members I previously listed have been identified. All passengers on the craft are deceased. We extend our deepest condolences. Personnel will be arriving at your address shortly for additional insight. Is there anything else I can do for you at this time?"

"Um, no. Thank you," I said, still in shock.

"Certainly. God bless you."

The operator hung up. I couldn't believe what I just heard. It didn't feel real, it couldn't be real. 'Why didn't I think to call them earlier in the day?' I lamented.

I had figured that they were trying to get settled and got caught up with other activities. I figured I'd contact them the next morning. But I guess they never even made it.

I had just lost the cornerstone of my home. This home was nothing without them. I was nothing without them. A man doesn't make his family, the family makes him; and without them who was I? All the importance and responsibility I had just vanished along with them.

'I will never get another family like this. I can't start another family. I don't want another family. I want *my* family. What am I supposed to do?' I said to myself as I collapsed to the floor.

2 Weeks Later

It was now two weeks since the crash and two days since the funeral for my wife and kids. It was a difficult situation for me. On top of losing my immediate family, it was also awkward as hell with Eubi's family. I had never been particularly close with any of them; especially my in-laws. So despite all these years, they were merely just strangers to me now. They were supportive and I promised to try and keep in occasional contact with them just in memory of the woman I loved; Eubi. But deep down I knew I probably wouldn't. Just too painful.

Life had been very lonely for me since losing them. I was still in the Kaminawa family house, but now it felt so empty. The bed I shared with Eubi had too much space. No more loudness from Ruko running around and getting toys all over the floor. No more Myna getting annoyed with me for kissing and hugging her. (She was starting to get to 'that age' where she felt awkward.) And no more Luna closing her door on me when I tried to enter without permission and slamming it when I would tell her, "No boys allowed."

It was all just gone. It felt as if I'd lost all my values as a father and a husband. The house was silent. No more cooked meals, just takeout. I even started to go out drinking more often. Even more than I ever had in college.

I had already contemplated suicide multiple times in the past few weeks but I never gained the true courage to do so. I knew Eubi would be turning in her grave if she knew of these intrusive thoughts of mine.

I'm not too close with my own family either. My family was just that, my family...

The only thing I had now was my job, and my best friend Akane.

Akane called me up after work to have dinner at a bar restaurant with him one night and I agreed. Although I didn't really like being out much anymore, I figured Myna was mocking me from above for being a loner. Plus I was only gonna get more take out anyway. So we met at around seven in the evening.

"So dude," Akane asked. "How ya been holding up?"

"Dude, is that even a question," I replied.

"Sorry man. You know I've never been good at these type of things." Akane admitted.

"Neither have I!" I shot back

"Well, I'm glad you came out tonight, man. It's not good to hole yourself inside alone during times like this."

"Thanks for inviting me. Otherwise I probably wouldn't have had an outing for the rest of my life!"

"Well man, if you ever feel lonely at any time, just swing by my place. You don't even have to call me ahead or anything, just come. I'm gonna give you an extra key to my place!"

"Thank, but I can still take care of myself!"

"Well that's a good sign! My guy is still enough of himself to be an asshole!" Akane joked.

"I just don't know how I'm supposed to go on living."

"I can understand. I might not be married and I only have two sons, but if I lost them, my world would definitely be shattered. At times like this, all you can really do is place it in God's hands."

I've never been the religious type, so when he mentioned God, I kinda cringed a little.

"Wow, my first date since I lost my wife and you bring up God, you're doing a great job man!"

"My bad, man," Akane apologized. "I forgot you were never the religious type. It's beneficial to have something to believe in at times like this, ya know?"

"I actually do believe in God, or the higher power or whatever, I just don't believe in religion. It's like an international scam generated from thousands of years back!"

"I can understand your feelings," Akane admitted. "Some religions can be very *pushy*."

"And judgmental. And very contradictive!" I added.

"Agreed, but you just gotta find a way to trust in your values and beliefs whether your part of a congregation or not."

"Thanks. I'll toss it around. But I didn't come out tonight to talk about religion. I came to get drunk and to eat. You're paying right?"

"You're kidding, right?"

"Bro, you invited me on a date and you ain't gonna even pay?" I joked with him.

"Stop calling this a date. We're in public ya know!"

"My bed is a little lonely these nights now!" I continued to mess with him.

"SHUT UP, WEIRDO!"

We laughed together then ate and drank the night away.

•

Saturday went by in a flash. I didn't do much of anything. I did however spend the day reminiscing, crying, more crying and just walking around the hollow house. Sunday morning came and went. The afternoon started to sweep in so I decided to go out and get some ingredients to cook a meal for myself for dinner.

I went to the local grocery market. I couldn't help notice the families out shopping together. I felt jealous watching the kids being pests to the parents who were trying to shop.

While in the vegetable aisle, my attention was directed to a handsome, well-dressed male.

"Do you like what you see?" Renji asked.

"Sorry, sorry. My, my apologies!" I stammered.

"No worries," Renji smiled. "You're not too bad yourself!"

"Thank you, but I don't really go that way."

"Relax, just two men complimenting each other. Nothing wrong with that."

"Yeah, I guess."

It was a very awkward interaction. The guy started to walk up closer to me.

"My name's Renji, nice to meet you!"

He held out his hand and I shook it.

"Same here. I'm Yokami."

"Yokami... I like that name!"

"Uh, thanks."

"Yokami, you look like you've been through a lot."

"Sheesh, you just complemented me but I guess I must look pretty bad."

"Feel free to correct me if I'm wrong."

"Well you're not entirely wrong."

"I know we just met, but would you be comfortable sharing with me?"

"Honestly, I don't."

"That's fine," Renji said. "I understand."

Finally I said, " Well, I lost some loved ones not too long ago."

"Wow, I'm sorry for your losses, Yokami. I may be able to help you."

"Unless you have some magic abilities to bring them back to life, I don't think there's much you can do for me."

"Well I wouldn't exactly call it magic, but I would call it a miracle."

"You're joking right? Like, you *are* joking?"

He smiled a bit,and pulled a card out of his front suit pocket to hand to me.

"Give me a call later, Yokami. We can discuss things in more detail privately!"

Then he turned and walked away.

I looked at the card. Printed on it in black bold letters was: AternuS Corporation. Renji's name was on it. His title was CEO & Product Developer. I had a feeling he was rich. The card also contained a slogan:

The soul is fragile, but a diamond is durable. Life may be temporary, but DIAMONDS are forever.

11

DIAMONDS ARE FOREVER
(PART II)

A day had passed since my interaction with Renji and it was been the only thing on my mind for the last twenty four hours. Was he actually capable of bringing my family back to me? I know it's 2035, but I didn't think technology has gotten that advanced. I can't deny that I was highly considering it. He didn't seem all that shady and his response seemed pretty genuine. I looked at his card all day at work. I continued to reread it over and over.

The soul is fragile, but a diamond is durable. Life may be temporary, but DIAMONDS are forever.

When I got home I decided to meet up with Akane at the bar. I just needed someone to talk to about this.

"Don't tell me you actually believe that bullshit!" Akane blurted out. "It's a total scam!"

"I know it doesn't sound all that realistic, but you miss every shot you don't take!"

"Yeah, but trusting some guy you just met who says he can bring your family back to life is not a shot to take."

"He seemed real genuine when he offered it to me though. He owns the company and I believe he designed whatever he's offering himself!" I insisted.

"Yokami, look, I get it man. But you're gonna have to learn to accept your family's passing. I know it's hard. I know it's been some time now. I'm not saying that you have to rush the grieving process, but eventually you have to move to the acceptance stage."

"COME ON! You're being so negative about it man!"

"I'm not being negative," Akane said. "I'm just being realistic and cautious; something *you* need to be."

Things got quiet at the table for a moment. After about three minutes, Akane broke the silence.

"Okay, let's say this Renji guy and AeternuS can really bring your family back somehow, someway. I'm not even gonna say back to life because a human cannot be brought back to life, but if he can do some weird shit with some crazy technology, who's to say that your family will even come back the same? After all, they died in a plane crash."

"I know. I've already considered all of those things. But it would give me a reason to continue living," I said.

"Keyword being: *you*, Yokami. Who's to say that your family would even want to be brought back? You can't cheat death and, most importantly, you can't play God."

"I know, but I just can't continue to live like this. When you get so used to living in a house with a wife, a woman I'd been with since freshman year in college, and three kids, I've watched grow up, it's not easy."

"I understand. I do," Akane empathized. "Although I don't exactly agree with it, you're my best friend and I'll support you if this is something that you really need to do. I'm gonna do some digging on this company first though, if that's cool with you."

"Sure. Thanks for the support!" I said enthused.

"On another note, have you heard about that boy, Kyomi? You know the one from your neighborhood that went missing over a month ago?"

"I haven't been keeping up," I admitted. "I don't know the family directly but I feel for them. Kyomi was a quiet, but good kid. I used to pass by him a lot on my way to work. He always waved."

"It's really a shame. All the people coming up missing recently. I pray they get found."

•

The next morning I called Renji and I told him how I still had some doubts. He was relatively understanding but convinced me to come to the company for an event they were having at twelve in the afternoon. He said that I didn't have to agree to anything up front. It would just be a tour and the opportunity to see 'proof' of their work.

Once the afternoon rolled around, I drove to AeternuS. It wasn't too far, but it was definitely secluded in a private area. The building itself had a very modern design.

Once I was approved by security, I went in and signed in with the receptionist. Renji was already there waiting for me. We greeted each other and he started to give me a tour around the facility. When I tell you this place was big, I mean BIG.

I was trying to not only keep up with everything he was showing and explaining to me, but also trying to maintain a close distance. I could tell how easy it would be to get lost in there. I could see where the whole 'diamond' inference came from. The product itself was actually a diamond shaped device that acts as a 'brain' for the clone. That's right *clone*!

If they had body parts of the dead person to salvage for design inspiration they would use them. But if they didn't, they would just take images of the person to scan into their system for the bionic design.

Within their program they would input up to two thousand 'quals.' Quals are essentially features to make the clone as human and realistic as possible. These quals included things such as skills, expressions, personality traits, emotions, etc.

"So, how are you liking the tour so far?" Renji asked.

"It seems pretty legit so far," I said. "I can see the knowledge and the money in play."

"So are you still interested in bringing your family back? I know you said they died in a plane crash, but as you can see we don't actually need body parts, they just help us give a more dynamic feel."

"I don't know. I definitely want to but something about it feels wrong. I just don't know what. But I do want my family back."

"Well, to convince you a little more, I'm gonna give you an inside look on one of our latest projects."

An employee brought out someone. I couldn't actually believe my eyes. The person they brought out was none other than Kyomi Matsukoto. It was definitely him. There was no denying that. But he was slightly different. He looked more muscular and athletic than before. He was also taller."

"What the hell, didn't he just go missing some time ago?" I asked, confused.

"Yes, the actual Kyomi is dead," said Renji. "But this is his clone. We were actually able to salvage some of his body parts. However, the requestee's didn't want that. They wanted a Kyomi that the world had never seen before."

Despite the slight changes to some of his physical features, it was most definitely Kyomi. It wasn't just his physical features, but even his whole demeanor, his whole aura was different than what I remembered.

"What exactly do you mean by requestee's, if I may ask?"

"The people that paid," Renji said. "Yokami, I'm gonna let you in on a little secret. Everyone coming here isn't like you. You're coming in with an innocent, moral request. But you'd be surprised to see how many people come in here with a twisted request."

I looked puzzled.

Renji continued, "Take this boy for example. The truth is that he was actually murdered by his own parents. They were *tired* of him, or so they claim, so they killed him. They buried his body and filed him as 'missing' so they wouldn't look guilty. Then, after a couple of weeks, they came here. We've been working on him for the last few weeks and he's now complete. They'll be coming by to pick up their new son soon."

"What the hell?" I said, stupefied.

"Yokami, why do you think they came here?"

"Well, I guess they'd eventually become prime suspects after a while, right?"

"Partially, but their real goal was to get a whole new son. You know, the son they always dreamed of. The son that's tall, athletic, and muscular. He will now be playing sports and getting all the girls in school. If they only cared about being caught, they would've just chosen to bring him back the same as when was when he was alive. But no. They decided to create a vision of what they had always wanted Kyomi to be."

"So you guys knew he was killed, knew who killed him and you didn't think to let authorities know?"

"We have a strict non-disclosure with our customers that works both ways. We won't discuss their business as long as they don't discuss ours. But I decided to make an exception for you today. Besides, much of our funding when we first began came from the Japanese government themselves."

"Our government?"

"Yes. We have many politicians, government officials, rich people, and famous people who come here to clone others. At times they even come to get cloned themselves. Our market is growing rapidly and pretty soon we'll be expanding into partnerships with foreign countries and other very powerful entities.

"Like who?" I asked.

"Well, basically, all of them. Government, Political, Military, Rich, Elite, Famous, Drug, Crime, Kingpins; all of them."

"So you'll be going public with this soon?"

"Those are our key and target customers regardless of whether or not we actually go completely public. My stakeholders are ready to launch publicly, but I'm attempting to halt that for the moment. This is something that could get really dangerous if we simply offered it to everyone."

"You say that as if it already isn't dangerous. All those people for your market you named are some of the worst kinds of human being to ever exist. Make it make sense!"

"You're right, Yokami, those are some of the worst people. But the everyday people are just as cruel, if not more. Take the Matsukoto's for example. They were just your everyday family who decided to kill their son and recreate him into their own desired image. They'll be picking him up today and returning home as if nothing ever happened. They'll relate the tragic story of almost loosing their son but announce that he's back and better than ever. No one is the wiser. He'll go back to high school, go to prom, graduate, go to college and even potentially get married. Also, they are not the first. They just happen to be the most recent."

I couldn't even believe what I'd just witnessed and all of what I had just heard. I was mind-blowing to think that this was actually real and not a dream.

"Personally, I don't encourage the idea of bringing this to the total public eye," Renji continued. "The Matsukoto's and others are a perfect example of the dangers of putting this in the hands of everyone. We're giving people the power to play God. And if we give it to everyone, the human race might be extinguished until most of us are living as AI. I respect your righteousness. That's why I want to offer you this opportunity to be with your family again. And I want to give it to you for free!"

"Really? For free?" I was stunned.

"Yes. This is truly the opportunity of a lifetime. The Matsukoto's used a good chunk of their life savings to create their son's clone."

Despite being very desperate, I was still reluctant to take Renji's offer. I just wasn't sure if it was the right thing to do as whole or the right thing to do for myself.

Renji added, "I'll make another deal with you! If you don't like what you see, or if you're just not feeling right about the way things turn out, I'll personally see to the disposal of the replicas myself."

Selfishness got the better of me. I agreed to Renji's terms and conditions. During the signing paperwork and while filling out the NDA, I was genuinely excited and happy but still unsure if I had made the right decision.

Renji escorted me out of the building. As we shook hands, he said he would fast track my 'order' and would personally contact me when it was time to pick up my 'family.' He said the whole process would take about two or three days.

I left and went back to my lonely home still wondering if I had truly made the right decision. But I'd be lying if I said I wasn't excited. I was already building my plan; the plan I somehow thought would be flawless.

Unfortunately, I was about to learn the repercussions that I was now facing.

The soul is fragile, but a diamond is durable. Life may be temporary, but DIAMONDS are forever.

12

DIAMONDS ARE FOREVER
(PART III)

The next few days went by quickly. I went to work as normal, showered, cooked some dinner, watched some movies, and anticipated my family being back home. It was all I could really think about for three days.

How would they be? Would they be like my real family? I also couldn't stop thinking about how I could be discreet with it. It was definitely something I wasn't ready to tell both our families about yet. And it's definitely not something I wanted to make super obvious to my neighbors. I didn't feel like explaining how my dead family is back alive; at least not right away.

The day had finally come. The day for me to go and pick them up. When I got to AeternuS, I excitedly went up the elevator to meet with Renji.

"Well Yokami, how are you feeling today?" Renji asked.

"I'm excited and nervous," I admitted. I really was a bundle of mixed emotions.

"Don't be nervous," Renji assured me. "This is what you wanted and something I truly believe you deserve."

"Don't get me wrong," I said. "I'm really happy, but I just can't help but feel as if I'm replacing my family in a way. They'll never be my real family and I pray they aren't angry with me!"

"Well of course they will never be able to be the original thing," Renji said. "But we've designed them to be the most realistic versions as possible; virtually to the point of absolute perfection. And I promise, they will not be angry with you!"

When the clones were brought out to me, I immediately started to cry. They replicated my family as I've always known them. Eubi had the gorgeous, long, dark brown hair, and the beautiful small mole near the bottom of her face by her lip. Luna has the gorgeous black hair with bangs, and the small mole like her mother. Myna was still as small and as cute as ever. Ruko had his spiky hair and baby face.

"DADDY! I missed you!" Ruko shouted.

"Sweetie! It's so good to see you!" Eubi beamed.

"Hi Daddy!" Myra smiled.

"Sup Dad!" spouted Luna.

They all greeted me with the same tone and same expressions that they've always had. I ran to them and grouped them all in for a big hug. I cried. Seeing all of them and hearing their voices was overwhelming.

"I... I've missed you all too!" I cried.

Together, we all went down to the lower level to exit the building. Eubi was softly barking orders like she always did. Ruko was being a menace to Myna. Luna was being an annoyed pre-teen as usual. It felt just like old times; as if nothing had happened or changed at all.

As they were all preparing to get in the car, I had my final conversation with Renji before going home with my 'family.'

"Renji," I said. "I wasn't exactly sure about this, but this is absolutely incredible. This is beyond my expectations.

Thank you! Thank you from the bottom of my heart! Are you sure you don't want any form of payment?"

"Of course not," Renji replied. "I meant what I said. Don't worry about it!"

"Wow, are you sure it isn't a good idea to open this to the public? This could truly change lives. Imagine if people could still get to be with the one they love even after death!"

"Again Yokami, not everyone that comes here is only looking to bring back the one they love. You know the expression, you give a man an inch and they will take a mile. Besides, the original purpose of this was supposed to be used for entertainment purposes only. Unfortunately our biggest customers come here with more than the idea of entertainment. You've only seen one example."

I nodded.

"Enjoy this gift, Yokami. But keep in mind that they are still technology. They will never truly be the family you once had despite having pretty much all the internal and external features of your original family members."

"I'm already aware, Renji. And I promise, I won't."

"Also, we're giving you a tablet. With this device you can see where they are at all times. You can see when they experience a change in emotions, when they are hurt."

I nodded again accepting the tablet.

Renji continued, "And although it's highly unlikely, in the event they get dangerous for some reason, you can place them in temporary sleep mode. That will shut off the diamond core that keeps them functioning with just one tap. Good luck to you, Yokami!"

Renji and I shook hands once more then parted ways. I got in the car to drive home. I told my family that I was going to cook dinner for everyone tonight, to which they responded excitedly. We drove home as the beautiful family that we had always been...

•

5 Weeks Later

The first four weeks were a blast. It felt so real, so natural. Everything felt like it had been before; so much to the point that I started to forget the fact that they were actually dead.

We had dinner like usual, we laughed like usual, we watched movies together like usual, and I went to work like usual. The only things different were that my wife couldn't go to work or go shopping like she used to. The kids couldn't go to school like they used to. They all couldn't go outside at all to be exact. I told them it wasn't safe for them.

Initially, they didn't seem to mind. It wasn't until the fifth week when things took a turn.

I was at work when I got an alert on AeternuS tablet. I took it with me everywhere. The alert showed that Luna and Myna had gotten outside of the house. I started freaking out. I told my boss I had an emergency at home and ran out of work and back to the house.

Thankfully my job was only about fifteen minutes from my home, but even that felt like too much time. When I got to my driveway, I looked at my tablet and saw that Luna and Myna were located at my neighbors house. I looked over to see them standing at Miss Furukawa's porch talking to her. Miss Furukawa looked absolutely shocked as she was standing there talking to them.

"GIRLS! GET IN THIS DAMN CAR RIGHT NOW!" I yelled at them angrily.

Both girls obeyed and got in the car. I drove back across the street to our driveway. We got inside the house and I was absolutely livid at them.

"What the hell, girls! I thought I told you guys about going outside. It's too dangerous!"

"We just went outside. Nothing happened to us," Luna argued. "Excuse us for being tired of being cooped up in this house!"

"I figured what was the harm of letting them go out once," Eubi said. "You keep saying it's dangerous outside but yet they're okay. You say it's dangerous, but what out there is dangerous? You won't tell us the truth!"

"Listen, if *any* of you were to be caught outside, it would cause too much conflict. It could put this family in jeopardy and we could lose everything. We won't be able to be a family anymore if anyone sees you all!"

Myna started crying. Luna stomped upstairs. Eubi took Ruko and walked away from the table.

•

I got no sleep at all that night. The next day at work I could only think about how Miss Furukwawa had seen the girls. I worried what she might do. I kept thinking about how the hell I could explain this to her.

I was able to get through my shift with no issues at home. I kept checking the tablet all day making sure that there were no other problems.

On my way home, I picked up some takeout. When I entered the house, it was very quiet.

"I'm home," I sang out. "I've got takeout!"

No one answered, so I plopped the takeout bags on the kitchen counter and turned toward the dining room to discover my whole family seated quietly around the dining room table.

In the middle of the table was the head of Miss Furukawa. My family all had blank, heartless expressions on their faces. They all turned their heads slowly to look at me.

"We got rid of her sweetie," Eubi announced.

"She won't cause any problems for us father," Luna conformed coldly.

"We can stay a family forever," Myna added.

I couldn't believe what I was seeing. They actually murdered Miss Furukawa. I started to panic. I grabbed the tablet and started to frantically press the button for them to shut down but the button wasn't working. I had no idea why. It was basically frozen.

"You're not trying to turn us off, are you father?" Luna questioned in a creepy, deadpan tone.

"N... no... no, of course not!" I stuttered.

•

Eight weeks have passed since I lost my family; and no these people, or better yet these *things* don't count. They are *not* my family. I lost them a long time ago now.

These 'fakes' have moved on from murdering Miss Fururkawa as if it's a normal everyday thing. They have absolutely no remorse.

I feel like I've lost all control while they've gained it. They still smile and laugh. They go about their daily routines and have not gone outside again. That part is good. But they keep boasting about our 'family.'

However, my original family would've *never* done anything as heinous as this. While I recognize they are AI and they aren't supposed to be flawless, shouldn't they adhere to basic human morals?

I've been trying to play it off for the sake of my own safety. I don't trust them and I believe that the moment I start to show too much resentment they'll finish me off; just like Miss Furukawa.

I contacted Renji about disposal, but I haven't received a response yet. I don't know how much longer I can wait. I've been tempted to 'dispose' of them myself, but I just can't bring myself to do it. I know they aren't actually my family, let alone real humans, but I just can't. They look too much like my them. Someone else has to do it.

My fear is that I don't know how much longer they'll stay in check. They murdered once with no remorse, I'm sure they could easily do it again. My neighbors are not safe and *I'm* not safe. I'm not even comfortable being in this house anymore; but I earned this.

Temptation, greed, and selfishness got the best of me. Now, I'm paying the price for attempting to play God. I've been trying everyday to shutdown their core with the tablet, but I'm having no luck. I not sure know why I can't. I believe they must be aware of this function and have somehow shut it off themselves. I'm starting to wonder if they can even be disposed of at this point.

Maybe this *will* lead me to my death. Then at least I can be with my actual family!

The soul is fragile, but a diamond is durable. Life may be temporary, but DIAMONDS are forever.

About the Author

Milo Zephyr is a graduate of Flint Genesee Job Corps. He spent two years in the Naval branch of the military as a personnel specialist. He's had a lifelong interest in horror that began around age seven. Milo began writing stories in the fourth grade and been hooked ever since.

Dubbed the Capricious Commander of Creepy, Milo Zephyr holds nothing back when it comes to literary lynching. Milo is the youngest author to sign with the Volossal Publishing label.